24

NOWHERE

MAY -- 2022

24 Hours in NOWHERE

DUSTI BOWLING

STERLING CHILDREN'S BOOKS

New York

STERLING CHILDREN'S BOOKS
New York

An Imprint of Sterling Publishing Co., Inc.
1166 Avenue of the Americas
New York, NY 10036

This 2020 edition published by Sterling Publishing Co., Inc.

Text © 2018 Dusti Bowling
Cover and interior art © 2018 João Neves

ISBN 978-1-4549-4016-6

Distributed in Canada by Sterling Publishing Co., Inc.
c/o Canadian Manda Group, 664 Annette Street
Toronto, Ontario M6S 2C8, Canada
Distributed in the United Kingdom by GMC Distribution Services
Castle Place, 166 High Street, Lewes, East Sussex BN7 1XU, England
Distributed in Australia by NewSouth Books
University of New South Wales, Sydney, NSW 2052, Australia
For information about custom editions, special sales, and premium and corporate purchases,
please contact Sterling Special Sales at 800-805-5489 or specialsales@sterlingpublishing.com.

Manufactured in Canada

Lot #:
4 6 8 10 9 7 5 3
06/21

sterlingpublishing.com

Cover and interior design by Ryan Thomann

For Zach: loving husband; dedicated father; motorcycle enthusiast; idea guy

Saturday 5:00 PM

BO TAYLOR HELD MY FACE ONE INCH FROM

the jumping cholla. "Eat it, Gus," he commanded.

I shook my head as much as I could with Bo's vise-like grip in my hair.

"You think you can get away with what you just pulled?" Bo squeezed my hair tighter.

I grimaced. "I was just hoping I could."

Bo let out a shrill laugh and put more pressure on the back of my head. "That's hilarious."

For those not familiar with things out here in the hideously hot, dry desert of southern Arizona, a jumping cholla is a cactus so nasty, it has a reputation for attacking unsuspecting people by leaping onto them— more rabid animal than plant. It then locks itself into place with spines that curve like hooked vampire teeth as they sink into its victim's skin.

I'd had plenty of cholla in my feet. A cholla in my mouth was something I'd never expected, since I didn't usually walk around the desert with my tongue dragging on the ground.

"Eat it now, Gus," Bo ordered again, pushing my face closer to the frightening barbs. I stared down at my shattered spaghetti sauce jar of water. My mouth felt as dry as the ground that had been wet only ten seconds ago.

I compared our feet. Next to my kids' size three Family Dollar clearance sneakers, Bo's heavy motorcycle boots looked like they belonged on the feet of a giant—a mean, ugly giant with blond hair and pork-and-beans-sprinkled-with-chewing-tobacco breath. Not a pleasant combination. I doubted they'd ever make a mouthwash with that flavor.

I tried to formulate an escape plan in my head using the information I had.

Bo Taylor: a thirteen-year-old in the body of an eighteen-year-old with the mind of an eight-year-old.

Me: a thirteen-year-old in the body of an eight-year-old with the mind of an eighteen-year-old. At least I liked to think so—I mean about the mind thing, not the body thing. The body thing sucked.

Bo's cronies: Matthew Dufort and Jacob Asher. Not quite as big or mean as Bo. I could have maybe fought off one of them. For about two seconds. The three of them would take me down in under one.

Someone who might help me: Uh . . . Not in this town. Not out here. Out here, we were all on our own. Out here, in the least livable town in the United States, Bo was the lord and I was the fly.

So, yeah, still no good plan how to get out of eating the cholla and experiencing the most excruciating pain of my life, either when it went in or when it came out. I couldn't decide which would be worse. Then again, it would probably cling to the inside of my mouth and get stuck, unable to make its way down my throat. That, in some way, was a comfort.

"Let him go, Bo," a voice said from behind me. Not just any voice—an unusually deep, raspy voice. A voice I would recognize anywhere.

"Go away, Rossi. This doesn't concern you," Bo said.

"Yeah, this doesn't concern you," Matthew echoed Bo.

"Yes, it does," Rossi said. "You're angry I beat you again this morning, so you're taking it out on someone smaller and weaker than you. You're pathetic."

I pursed my lips. "Not *that* much smaller and weaker," I muttered.

"*You're* pathetic," Bo said. "Why don't you do us all a favor and go back to Mexico?"

I gritted my teeth. I tried to turn my head out of his grasp, but he gripped my hair tighter.

"Are you for real?" Rossi said. "You do realize not all brown people are Mexican, don't you?"

"Oh, excuse me," Bo crooned. "Then go back to the reservation."

"Yeah, go back to the Navajos," Jacob added, and I heard him and Matthew snicker together. What a couple of suck-ups.

I ground my teeth so hard, it was a wonder they hadn't already turned to dust like everything else around us. "She's Tohono O'odham, not Navajo," I grumbled.

Bo smacked the side of my face with the hand that didn't have my hair in a death grip. "No one asked you, loser, and no one cares, so shut up."

"Let him go," Rossi said again.

"You know what?" Bo said. "I'm glad you're here so you can watch this wimp eat this cactus."

He pushed on the back of my head. It took all my strength to fight against the pressure. My face twisted up from the effort—it felt and probably looked like a habanero pepper by now. The tip of my nose pressed into the cholla, and I did my best not to cry out.

"Stop it!" Rossi cried. "Now!"

"What do you care anyway?"

"I care about nasty ogres torturing the meek to compensate for their insecurities."

Bo was quiet for so long that I risked turning my head slightly to look up at him. His face alternated between confused and furious as he attempted to process what she'd just said. He glanced at Jacob and Matthew like he was looking for help, but they didn't have any to offer. He finally settled on the brilliant response of "Shut up!"

Bo squeezed my hair so tightly, I thought there was a good possibility I'd end up needing to borrow one of my grandma's wigs when he was done. I pondered for a moment how I might look with a red bouffant. Not great.

"Don't tell me what to do!" Bo screamed at Rossi, the spit flying from his mouth flashing in the bright, hot August sun, some of it landing on my cheek. I wiped at it. Gross. Spit shouldn't have color.

"Unless," Bo grinned a grin that could have killed a hundred fluffy puppies, "you want to make a trade."

"I don't have anything to trade," Rossi said.

Bo laughed. "Oh yes, you do." He finally relaxed his grip on my hair enough that I could turn my head to see her.

She stood there, still in all her motorcycle gear, her helmet gripped in her right hand hanging by her side, Loretta standing next to her. Rossi's long, dark hair was pulled back in a ponytail, all messy and sweaty from the races that afternoon. A lot of it had come loose, and one strand was plastered to her cheek. Her brown eyes glittered in the brilliant sunlight.

Rossi looked down at Loretta. Then at Bo. Then at me. "No."

In the short time Rossi had lived in Nowhere, she hadn't spoken a single word to me. I wasn't sure she had ever even looked at me until this moment. I knew she would never give up Loretta. Not for a useless wimp like me. And I wouldn't want her to, anyway. Nope. I'd be drinking my generic macaroni and cheese through a straw from now on.

"Fine." Bo retightened his grip on my hair. "Open your mouth, loser." When I didn't, he pushed my lips into the cactus. The needles punctured the tender skin. Against all my willpower, I whimpered. Man, I whimpered in front of Rossi. I officially hated Bo with the strength of all the muscles I wished I had.

"I'll trade my gear." Rossi's voice shook.

"Won't fit." Bo pushed harder on my head.

"You can sell it."

"How many girls race around here? I mean besides you, you freak?"

"Yeah, you freak," Jacob said. I rolled my eyes. Did either of those guys have an original thought in their heads?

"I have some money," Rossi said. "I have eighteen dollars at home."

"Come on," Bo said. "His life is worth more than that."

"Don't do it, Rossi," I managed to mumble through pierced, already swelling lips. "It won't kill me."

"I guess we'll find that out." Bo pushed me deeper into the cactus.

I couldn't find the strength to hold it in any longer. I screamed.

ignominy: public shame; disgrace

I knew a lot of vocabulary words. Vocabulary words were just about the most important things in the world to me. And not because I found learning them to be a thrilling adventure. Vocabulary words were going to save my life. That was, if my life didn't end right here and now.

"Fine!" Rossi shouted. "Stop it!"

Bo pulled my head back, and some of the needles

ripped out of my lips, causing me to cry out again. One small cholla ball stayed stuck in my cheek. I had no clue how to remove it without gloves or pliers, so I stood there with it glued to my face like an idiot.

"Give her to me." Bo practically salivated.

"Don't—" I started to say, but Bo pushed me away with one hand and I flew back into the dirt on my butt. Jacob and Matthew laughed.

Rossi walked Loretta to Bo and shoved her into his hands. I worried she might cry. She didn't. Instead, she told Bo, "You're going to embarrass yourself at that camp."

Bo clucked his tongue. "At least I'll be going to that camp." He ran his hands over Loretta in a way that made me shudder. "You'll never beat me again, Rossi. And I think I'll rename her." Bo pulled out a pocket knife and started scraping at the letters Rossi had engraved into the handlebars. "Loretta's a stupid name for a motorcycle."

When Bo was done erasing the name from the dirt bike, he scratched his chin and pretended to think. "Hm. For a new name, how about . . ." Rossi watched Bo, her glare slowly turning into a look of confusion, as he carved the letters T R A S H E E P into the front fender.

When he was done, Rossi looked up at him. "What's a trasheep?" she asked. "Is it some kind of animal?"

"Can't you read?" Bo spat at her. "It's a trash heap." He pounded his pointed finger on the fender. "Trash. Heap."

Then Bo put on his helmet and jumped up on the starter. The bike sputtered then died. He muttered something under his breath and jumped up on the starter again. The bike coughed and gave a loud popping sound. It died again. "Piece of garbage bike," Bo growled. He jumped up on the starter one more time and gave it a ton of gas. The bike roared to life, black smoke spewing from the exhaust pipe.

Bo rode off on Loretta, leaving Matthew and Jacob to figure out how to get three dirt bikes home with only two people. I imagined they'd be standing there awhile, scratching their empty heads.

I trailed behind Rossi through the desert. Her motorcycle boots crunched as she marched over the desiccated earth, her helmet gripped hard next to her side, her loose ponytail swaying with every step.

"I can't believe you did that," I said. She didn't respond. "I'm sorry, Rossi." She still didn't respond. She didn't look at me either, but that was probably for the best—that piece of cholla was still sticking out of my face, and I doubted anyone could take me seriously. Not that anyone *ever* took me seriously.

Rossi stopped, and I nearly ran into her. She whipped around and faced me. "Don't apologize," she snapped. "It was my choice. I did it."

"I don't know how, but I'll get your bike back for you."

"He'll never give it back."

"I'll buy it back. I'll get the money somehow."

"Don't you understand, Gus? It doesn't matter. He'll never give my bike back because the most important thing to him is winning. Not the camp. Not my dirt bike. It's winning. He knows I can't get another bike by tomorrow. Maybe not ever."

"I'll borrow money from someone to buy you a dirt bike."

"There's no way to get one by tomorrow."

"But what about your dad?"

"What about him?"

"Won't he be angry? Maybe he can get Loretta back for you."

"He doesn't have time to deal with this meaningless stuff."

"It's not meaningless," I insisted. "You can't give up. You have to go to that camp."

"I don't have to do anything. Someone else gets to go now."

"But you're the one who should be going. I still can't believe you did that. I mean, why? Why would you do such—"

Rossi suddenly reached out one motorcycle-gloved hand and yanked the cholla ball from my cheek. I let out a cry of pain and surprise.

"It's always best to remove it quickly when you don't expect it," she said. Then she scraped the cholla off her glove with her boot. She pulled off the glove and touched her bare finger to a bump on my lip. I couldn't believe Rossi was touching my lip. My habanero face got even hotter. "You'd better get home and take care of your face. You're getting all lumpy."

Great. Of all the things I'd ever hoped to be in front of Rossi:

Brave

Daring

Dauntless

Strong

Tall

Heroic

No. No, lumpy was never on the list. Unless we're talking about lumpy muscles.

She turned and walked away. I watched her, my face throbbing and itching and burning, until she disappeared into the shimmering brown heat. Then, shoulders slumped, I made my way to my trailer.

My grandma was sitting in her recliner as always, watching a talk show that consistently featured women getting into ridiculous fistfights over something point-less—usually a bald man with a beer belly and tattoos who may or may not have just gotten released from prison. This is what she did, day in and day out—"just starin' at four walls," as she put it.

monotony: lack of variety and interest;
tedious repetition and routine

Man, I hoped I wasn't facing a life of endless "just starin' at four walls." Anything but that.

"Hi, Grandma," I said through swollen, itchy lips.

She didn't answer. She rarely did when this partic-ular show was on, too mesmerized by the spectacle. Today I was glad for it, so I didn't have to explain why my face looked like I had a mutant case of chicken pox.

I made my way to the bathroom and turned on the faucet. I stuck my head under it and rinsed my hair and face with the warm water. I would have given anything for some cool water, but the coolest water in Nowhere was warm if you were lucky, hot if you weren't.

I gulped directly from the faucet until I couldn't stomach any more muddy-tasting water. Then I opened the tiny medicine cabinet. The downside of sharing a bathroom with your grandma—your toothbrush sits next to her dentures on the counter, your towels sit next to her adult underwear on the shelf, and the anti-itch ointment sits next to her corn remover in the medicine cabinet. I did my best not to touch the corn remover while I retrieved the anti-itch, like I was playing a game of Operation.

I slammed the medicine cabinet shut and stared at my puffy face in the mirror. I plucked the remaining needles from my cheeks and mouth, each of them holding on like my skin was trying to eat them. I blotted away the blood with a piece of toilet paper and examined the damage—at least the red spots didn't stand out too much against my perpetually sunburned skin. I ran a hand through my soaked black hair, which I cut myself with dull scissors, leaving it choppy and uneven.

I hated Bo Taylor. Not only had he mangled my face, he had humiliated me in front of Rossi. Now she wouldn't win like she was supposed to. She wouldn't get to go to that camp. She wouldn't get a brand new dirt bike. And Bo had her old dirt bike. Because of me.

nugatory: of no value or importance; worthless

"You worthless wimp," I said to myself in the mirror. "Worthless, worthless, worthless."

I huffed and cursed under my breath, squeezing anti-itch onto my face. "You better not be cursing in there!" I heard my grandma shout from the other side of the door (there must have been a commercial break).

I swear, the woman was like a cursing detector. No matter where I was or what I was doing, if I let out any kind of curse, even mumbled it under my breath, she was right there, ready to force-feed me a can of Brussels sprouts—the ultimate cursing punishment and the only vegetable in my diet.

"I'm not, Grandma!" I called back. "I'm going to the bathroom. I need my privacy."

"You got the trots again?"

I groaned. "No, Grandma. I do not have the trots." Why was she always so interested in discussing the status of my poop?

She was quiet, so I assumed she had left to go back

to her TV show. I checked my face in the mirror again and hoped the swelling would go down, then I peeked my head out the door. "Whatchya doin' in there?" she demanded, her face only about one inch from mine.

I shrieked and dropped the cream. "Nothing." I bent down to pick it up, hoping she wouldn't notice the lumps on my face.

She scratched at her head, her entire poufy red wig moving with the motion. "You getting some kind of rash?"

"Yes, I'm getting a rash. I think it's heat rash. It's hotter than a forest fire in hell today."

She stared at me, her wrinkled face all extra wrinkled up in a look of consternation, like she was trying to determine whether I had just cursed or not, her fingers probably itching for the can opener. "You ought to put some of my hemorrhoid cream on there," she finally said. "That'll take care of it."

"No, thank you. I'm fine," I said, instead of falling to my knees and screaming "NOOOOOOO!" like I wanted to.

"You better go to bed then so you're all rested up and feeling better for the first day of school on Monday." She tapped her leathery cheek.

It wasn't even six o'clock yet.

"Sure, Grandma." I stood on tiptoe and gave her a quick kiss on her cheek, then I made my way the two steps to my tiny bedroom. "Goodnight, then." I closed my door before she could say anything else.

I threw myself down on my musty bed and wiped the sweat from my forehead. The swamp cooler barely kept the trailer's temperature below ninety and, true to its name, turned the place into a total swamp.

I let my mind run. I wished there was some way for me to get Rossi's bike back, but the wishing wells in Nowhere were all filled to the brim with desert dust.

I SAT UP IN BED. THERE WAS REALLY ONLY

one thing I could do to get the bike from Bo—I'd have to buy it back. I hunted around my room for anything that might be of value—all I came up with were some old garage sale action figures that could be considered collector items by some people. But they weren't in the box. And they were dirty. And some were broken. Okay, they were complete garbage.

I had a few books: my thesaurus (I doubted I could pay anyone to take it), a sports book called *The Great Ones*, a book called *Our Cool Brain* about how cool the brain is (obviously), and an SAT prep book that was about ten years out of date. But most of my books were borrowed from the high school's library.

It probably wouldn't be a good idea to sell them. And who in Nowhere would want to buy a book anyway?

I had my clothes. But most third-graders didn't have any money. And, really, even if my clothes could fit someone older than that, I doubted I would be able to squeeze more than a quarter out of each piece.

The truth was I owned nothing valuable. A thirteen-year-old kid living in his grandma's trailer in the poorest town in Arizona isn't exactly rolling in it—unless *it* is thirty-year-old orange shag trailer carpet crawling with enough dust mites to take over the entire county.

I reached into my pants pocket. Well, maybe it wasn't *completely* true that I owned nothing valuable. I pulled out my pocket watch and ran a finger over the engraved initials: W.D.A. It had belonged to my great-grandfather, Fergus Foley. No one knew what the initials stood for. My grandma had given the watch to my father, and my father had given the watch to me. It was one of the only things he'd ever given me, and now it was the only thing I owned worth anything at all.

I shoved it back in my pocket. Last resort.

I'd just have to go to Bo and see if there was anything I could possibly do for him. Maybe I could do his homework for him for the year. Then again, I didn't think Bo really cared about his grades.

I could tutor him for the SAT. I picked up the preparation book I borrowed regularly from the high school's library. The test may have been nearly four years away, but I was already studying for it. Of course Bo probably cared about that as little as he cared about his grades. Kids like Bo didn't go to college; they dropped out of high school. Nowhere High School's graduation rate was proof of that—the worst in the whole country.

I continued thinking about ways to get Loretta back. Maybe I could be, like, some kind of minion for Bo. Lots of villains had minions. I wasn't completely sure what being a minion entailed, but I was positive I could handle doing it. I thumbed through my thesaurus as I lay back on my lumpy pillow.

minion: follower; crony; underling; slave

Yeah, I hated that idea. That idea was the worst. I slammed the thesaurus shut and got up from the bed. I peeked out my door to see what my grandma was doing. As though she could feel me spying on her, she called from the kitchen, "You want some beans?"

"No, thank you."

"You sure? I put my special seasoning in there," she said in her best I'm-trying-to-entice-you tone.

Grandma's special seasoning was a spice she always had on hand (that she got from the dollar store in Casa Grande) called Spepper. I looked at the ingredients list on the bottle one day, and it's literally just salt and pepper mixed together in one container. But Grandma thought it made everything taste better. Really, she was right.

"That sounds good, but I think I might be getting sick. Must be that rash. I think I have heatstroke. I'm really going to bed now. Definitely going to bed and won't be coming back out."

She stirred the pot of canned beans, her eyes still fixed to the TV in the living room. "Good night," she said without looking at me. Not even the threat of me dying from heatstroke could tear her away from the sight of one woman dragging another woman across a stage by her hair while an audience cheered her on.

I shut my door and locked it. I opened my pocket watch and checked the time—6:15. I wound it up and put it back in my pocket. Pulling open my bed-side table, I took out the only seven dollars I had and stuffed the money into my pants. Then I opened my bedroom window and climbed through it, dropping down onto the parched desert dirt.

The day was still blisteringly hot as I made my way to Bo's trailer, but I hadn't wanted to risk getting a jar of water from the kitchen and making my grandma suspicious. August was a brutal time of year in Nowhere, when the thermostat dropped to ninety only in the middle of the night. The daytime temperatures were unbelievable, much like the high school graduation rate.

I gazed up at Hollow Mountain hovering over me as I passed through "town." The town of Nowhere sat at the base of the mountain and consisted of a gas station with one pump, the Nowhere Market and Ostrich Farm, a scrapyard, Rusty's Motorcycle Shop (owned by a guy named Bud), a bar called Cal's, and a second bar called Better Than Cal's.

Better Than Cal's was started by Robert Norton who, obviously, hated Cal Bunker. The feud between the two bar owners was legendary in Nowhere, a town with no movie theater, no mall, no anything else worth doing, but yes, two bars. I kept expecting Cal to change the name of Cal's to "Better Than Cal's Serves Rat Poison" or "Better Than Cal's Can Kiss My Butt," but he hadn't yet. Cal's had the world's largest collection of rattlesnake skins—the walls were practically papered with them. Better Than Cal's had the world's largest collection of rattlesnake rattles, all hanging from the ancient wooden-boarded ceiling. So, in addition to the longstanding feud, it seemed the two were also embroiled in some kind of snake-off.

Of course we also had two schools—Nowhere Elementary and Nowhere High School. At Nowhere Elementary, the middle schoolers were lumped in with the elementary students, as there weren't enough of us to have our own middle school. This might have been nice for those kids who felt like they ruled the school in seventh and eighth grade, but I didn't rule over anything or anyone—even the third graders bossed me around. Probably because most of them were capable of beating me up.

As I passed by the deserted school, tripping every now and then over the crumbling asphalt of Nowhere's only paved road, I felt sick about school starting again on Monday—endless hours sitting in class listening to boring lessons, decades-old textbooks, brown cafeteria food, hardly anyone to sit with at lunch, and kids who bullied like they were training for the Bully Olympics.

foreboding: apprehension; anxiety; fear

My whole life was just one big sense of foreboding.

I neared Bo's trailer, the foreboding churning in my stomach like my grandma's mushy egg salad (made better with Spepper, of course), and my previously brisk steps slowed to a trudge. Who knew what new forms of torture Bo might devise for me?

I walked up the warped, split wooden steps and knocked on the peeling front door of the dilapidated trailer. I mean, no one in Nowhere had a particularly lovely place to live, but this . . .

squalor: filthiness; a state of being extremely dirty and unpleasant

A man's voice shrieked, "Bo! Get the door!"

"Geez, Jack!" I heard Bo shout. "I'm coming!"

The metal door screeched open, and then I was staring into Bo's face for the second time that day. I must have done gone and lost my mind, as my grandma would say.

"What do you want, cactus face?" Bo's scowl contorted into a twisted smile and he laughed. "I sure did a number on you, didn't I?"

My mouth was as dry as the splintery wood creaking under my feet. When I spoke, it came out as a pitiful hoarse whisper. "Bo."

He leaned down. "Yes?" he whispered, mocking me.

I cleared my throat and swallowed. "Can I please buy Rossi's bike back from you?"

"With what?"

"I have a little money."

"How much?"

"Seven dollars, but—"

Bo burst out laughing. "You're a funny guy, Gus. Hilarious."

"I can work off the rest. I can do anything."

"Unless you can magically come up with a lot more money, forget about it."

I reached into my pocket and felt the watch. Rossi had traded her most valuable possession for me. I held it out to Bo. "How about this? It's worth a lot of money. It's really old. It's an antique, and I know—"

Before I could finish, Bo smacked my hand from underneath, and the watch went flying onto the porch. I gaped, completely helpless, as it slipped between the wide slats in the dried-up boards and disappeared. "You're crazy if you think I'd trade a whole motorcycle for a piece of garbage like that, no matter what kind of fancy words you use to describe it."

I turned back to him. "Then what? What do I have to do? I'll do anything."

Bo pursed his chapped lips, squinted his eyes, and scratched his chin. Oh my gosh. Was that . . . stubble? "How about you eat that cactus?"

I tore my eyes away from Bo's intimidating chin. "If that's what it takes."

"No," said Bo. "Too easy. Bring me a rattlesnake's rattle you bit off with your teeth while it's still alive. I want to see it squirming in your mouth. No! Bring me fourteen live bark scorpions, and let me watch as they crawl all over your body. No! Bring me the hide of a coyote you killed and skinned with your bare hands. Then wear *its* head on *your* head like a hat. No!"

I took a deep breath and resisted the urge to roll my eyes. Actually, I *was* kind of impressed; with his limited brain power, he had quite the imagination. "What? I'll do whatever it takes."

He grinned and narrowed his eyes at me. "Bring me a piece of gold from Dead Frenchman Mine to buy it."

I laughed. "Yeah, right."

Bo continued grinning at me. "Yeah. Right."

My laughter faded. I took a step back. "That mine is a death trap."

"Well, you said you'd do whatever it takes." Yeah. Yeah, I did say that, but I didn't think even Bo Taylor would want me to actually, um, *die*.

Dead Frenchman Mine was Nowhere's biggest claim to fame. A few years ago, two guys who had recently left Better Than Cal's went in it and never came back out. A section of it caved in, killing both of them. Then last year another patron of Better Than Cal's went in there, hoping to find the Dead Frenchman treasure. He never came back out, either. A rotten beam had fallen on his head.

Hey, I just thought of a new name for Cal's: "People Who Drink at Better Than Cal's End Up Dead."

The deaths were all over the news, and for about five minutes everyone in the country was aware of this poor little nothing town in the middle of the desert called Nowhere—the poorest town in Arizona with hidden treasure in a deadly mine. That was when that reporter came here to interview people about all the drunk guys who had died in there. His newspaper then went on to rank Nowhere as the least livable town in the entire United States—whatever that meant. I guess we were all on the verge of death out here in Nowhere. It really wasn't *that* bad a place to live, though. When you think about it, Nowhere was the best at a lot of things: number one in poverty, number one in high school dropouts, number one in least livability, number one in drunken mine deaths. We tried not to let it all go to our heads.

Dead Frenchman Mine originally got its name around seventy years ago when a French guy by the name of William Dufort hid in there after stealing a pile of gold from his partner, a Mexican rancher by the name of José Navarro. I knew all about it because it was also the night my grandma's father got bitten by a rattlesnake and died in the desert. And that pocket watch that had just disappeared under the floorboards was the only thing he had on him when he died.

Anyway, the story goes that José shot William for stealing the gold and William shot him back. As José lay on his deathbed, he told the sheriff what happened. The sheriff traced William Dufort back to the mine, where he had hidden. William Dufort set off explosives, causing that section of the mine to cave in, killing both himself and the sheriff. A lot of people had tried to find William Dufort's body since then, hoping it would have the gold on it, but no one had ever succeeded.

So basically everyone who had entered the mine in the last seventy years had died an agonizing, suffocating, bone-crushing death. In a nutshell.

"Besides," I said, "there's no gold left in that mine. If there were, it would be swarming with treasure hunters." People were always willing to risk their lives for money.

"I guess you'll have to go check and find out. That is, if you want Rossi's bike bad enough." He eyed me up and down. "I think you do. It's so obvious you have the hots for her."

"I do not!" I declared. I resisted the urge to look left. I read in the brain book that a good way to tell if a person was lying was that they tended to look to the left. Then again, how would Bo Taylor possibly know that? I wasn't sure he was even literate, so I allowed my eyes to slowly wander in that direction.

Not that I had the hots for Rossi. *Please*. She constantly had helmet hair. Plus, she was always sweaty and dusty from racing. I mean, that's just gross.

"You do, too." Bo leaned into me and spoke low and slow through his filmy, yellow, brown-flecked teeth. His breath now smelled like Spam, which was possibly a step up from chewing tobacco and pork and beans, but still, I could never eat Spam again—and that cut out about twenty-five percent of my meals. "You love that Hopi Indian."

My heart beat violently, increasing in intensity as it moved from my chest into my head. That rushing sound filled my ears. "I told you. She's Tohono O'odham."

"And I told you." Bo smirked as he glanced down at my clenched fists. "I don't care."

He knew exactly what he was doing—trying to antagonize me into doing something foolish so he would have an excuse to pound on my head until I was about six inches shorter. I resisted the urge to attack. If I took a swing at Bo now, I would never get Loretta back. Because I'd already be dead. Or much shorter. I wasn't sure which was worse.

"How much gold?" I asked through grinding teeth.

Bo shrugged. "A big enough piece to pay for the bike."

I squinted at him. "That dirt bike is barely worth anything."

"I know." He laughed like this was all some big joke. "It's such a worthless trash heap."

I didn't point out that Rossi had beaten him several times on that worthless trash heap. "Fine. I'll do it. I'll go to the mine, but I want your word that if I succeed, you'll let me have the bike back."

"Shut the door before I beat your head in," I heard Jack call. I jumped at the threat, but Bo just glared at me.

Ever since Bo's mom had died and his dad had gone to prison, he had been living with his brother, Jack, in their trailer. Jack's toughness was renowned in Nowhere—he once raced (and won) with a broken wrist. He'd also spent a year at the Center, which definitely added to his brutal image. He didn't get sent there for anything he did here. You could do just about anything in Nowhere and get away with it. Jack had made the mistake of pulling his crimes in Casa Grande. There were a lot of rumors about what he did to get put in the Center for Youth, the massive juvenile detention center between here and Casa Grande. Some kids claimed he beat up the wrong person. Bo frequently had black eyes and bruises, so I knew Jack was capable of it.

Bo stuck out his bony hand, scarred from punching things (I think), which was at least twice the size of mine. "Deal." I shook it, doing my best not to grimace as he nearly crushed my fingers *to death*. Then he slammed the door in my face.

I massaged my throbbing hand as I squatted down in the dirt in front of his trailer and peered under the porch. It was stuffed, *stuffed,* like a stinking garbage burrito. I crawled through smelly, leaking trash bags and old newspapers and torn pillows. It was like a filth sauna under there, heated by steaming, sour beer bottles.

I finally reached the space where the watch had fallen through. I heard a rattling and froze. I knew that sound. Everyone who lived in the desert knew that sound. But I had no idea where it had come from. The snake could have been hiding in a rotten stuffed animal for all I knew.

I stayed still, sweat pouring down my face, and debated what to do: Continue sorting through this festering garbage heap and possibly die? Or call it a day and leave?

nincompoop: a foolish person

I raised a shaking hand and gently pushed aside a garbage bag. The rattling continued. I moved forward slowly and shoved away a couple of old dirt bike tires. And there was the watch, perched on top of a moldy towel. I moved slowly forward and grabbed it, then started backing up the way I'd come in. The air felt almost cool as I pushed myself out from under the porch, grateful I wasn't all pumped full of venom.

I examined my pocket watch. The glass hadn't

shattered as I'd expected it would have, but the backing had come loose. I moved it a little from side to side with my thumb, but it didn't come off completely. Maybe I could fix it. I stuffed the watch back in my pocket and left that horrible place.

OKAY, I WASN'T A STUPID PERSON. NO,

really. I wasn't. I know this is hard to believe, especially after what I just did, but I was actually the smartest person in my school. I knew this because my fifth grade teacher pulled me aside after we did our state testing to let me know I had the highest scores in the entire school, and I should really be in honors courses, but Nowhere Elementary had no honors courses, so, yeah, congratulations on being so smart.

Then she had gripped my shoulders so hard it hurt and whispered something to me I've never forgotten. "Your only hope, Gus, is the SAT. Do you hear me?" I had nodded. At the time I had no clue what the SAT was. The first thing that had popped into my mind was some top-secret organization that might kidnap me out of Nowhere, which would have been completely awesome. But the SAT is nowhere near that exciting. "Your only hope," she repeated.

I understood now what my fifth grade teacher had meant: In one year, I would be attending a high school with the lowest graduation rate in the country, no honors courses, and no extracurricular activities. My only hope for getting out of Nowhere was to ace the SAT, the standardized test used for college admission.

So, despite not being a stupid person, going into Dead Frenchman Mine was a really, *really* stupid thing to do.

Was all this worth risking my life?

I thought about Rossi shoving Loretta into Bo's hands. Of the look on her face when Bo rode off on her bike.

Yeah. Yeah, it was definitely worth it. Because . . .

equity: fairness; justness

Did I mention there was a vocabulary section on the SAT?

Someone had to fight for justice in Nowhere, so it might as well be me. It kind of made me feel like a superhero—a horribly undersized superhero. Like

Ant Man, but without the strength or skill. So yeah, an unskilled, weak, undersized superhero.

The sun was setting as I made my way back to town. There were other mines around Nowhere. I could even see Gold Tooth Mine off in the hazy distance—they had only mined enough gold out of it to make one gold tooth. There was also Darn Woman mine—so named because a "darn woman" staked the claim and mined a whole lot more out of it than a gold tooth's worth, causing every man within fifty miles to propose marriage to her. As far as I knew, she died very rich and very single.

Why hadn't Bo asked me to go into one of those mines? I knew why—because Dead Frenchman was the most dangerous. He probably figured I'd wimp out. Or worse.

While lost in my thoughts, my feet automatically carried me to Racetrack Basin, a place I visited nearly every day over the summer. I stood on a small hill at the edge of the basin and watched the last few stragglers racing the tracks, trails of pale desert dust following them like giant phantom snakes. I knew they were all hoping they would finally beat Rossi tomorrow. If I failed in my mission, they would.

No one else in the Sonoran Desert was crazy enough to race motorcycles in August. Only the kids in Nowhere were that reckless and bored. Nobody's parents seemed to care all that much, either. If a kid fainted and crashed or died of heatstroke, oh well. That was the risk you took. Collateral damage in the quest to make life suck just a little less.

Tomorrow was the most important race of the summer—the race that would determine, once and for all, who the best racer in Nowhere was. Bo had won the last two summers, and Rossi had been the first person to challenge him when she showed up this year. According to the leaderboards in the motor-cycle shop, whoever won tomorrow would take the summer. I knew Rossi would win if she could get Loretta back.

Everyone was shocked this year when it was announced that a mysterious sponsor had donated a brand new dirt bike for the winner. Not only that, but the winner would get to go to a special camp at world-famous Breaker Bradley's Motocross Training Facility, which was owned by the legendary Breaker himself. No prize had ever been offered like that before. Last year's winner was awarded a year of free Popsicles from the Nowhere Market and Ostrich Farm. But even that had been a step up from the previous year's prize:

a ten-dollar gift certificate to the scrapyard. I heard Bo got a few lug nuts and a rusty crowbar out of it.

The sky turned from pink to purple as I gazed out at the racers. One of the riders ate it on a jump, rolling end-over-end through the dirt. I was glad to see him get up. He seemed okay. I watched as the others turned a corner and hit the silt, one of them getting stuck, another toppling from something hidden underneath the powder. Racetrack Basin was a brutal track, mostly because it just wasn't maintained very well. Or, really, at all. It may very well have been the most rutted track in the world.

Over the years, hundreds of bored Nowhere kids had turned Racetrack Basin into quite a track, though. Young hands had transformed the flat, dry lake bed into whoops and jumps and sharp turns and berms and dips. It was extremely large, the entire course nearly two miles—twice as long as the average dirt bike track. That also meant it was difficult to see the riders when they were at the farthest point from the starting line, which was why I liked to sit up on the small hill on the far side of the track to watch the races.

Another rider turned a corner and accidentally hit the loose silt, sending up a giant dust cloud. He slowed way down and got stuck. Racetrack Basin was littered with silt pockets because it was a dry lake bed. The track that everyone stuck to was well compacted due to all the riding, but everywhere around the track were deep areas of loose silt that were near impossible to ride through. If you were stuck behind a bunch of riders with nowhere to pass, you didn't attempt to pass in the silt. Everyone avoided the silt, even Rossi.

I sighed as I gazed out at the riders. In a town where dirt bike racing was everything, not being a racer definitely made me a loser.

I continued on my way to the Nowhere Market and Ostrich Farm as the sky darkened and the air turned from scorching to stifling, the strange booming sounds of the ostriches getting louder with every step.

Now here's something important to know about Nowhere: about ninety percent of the people who live here have no choice. They're trapped. No money. No education. No family. Trapped. Like me. They would leave if they could. But the other ten percent of people—these people have *chosen* to live in Nowhere. And these are the people I liked to call weirdos. The owner of the Nowhere Market and Ostrich Farm, Mayor Handsome, definitely qualified as a full-fledged weirdo.

After I gulped down a massive amount of hot water from the rusty drinking fountain out on the front porch, I opened the door to the store, my belly burning. The bell jingled. Despite being the only grocery store in town, the Nowhere Market and Ostrich Farm had very limited supplies—some shelves of canned food, the adult diapers my grandma wore (and made me buy, often when other people were there to watch), toilet paper, common house tools. The very basics.

Oh, also shrimp. I had no idea where Mayor Handsome got the fresh shrimp he sold (he claimed they were fresh), because I'd never seen anyone delivering shrimp to the store. I once asked him what kind of shrimp they were. "Tasty shrimp," he had said. I asked him where they had come from. "From dee vater," was his reply. The only water in Nowhere was the kind that came out of the faucet or got flushed down the toilet, so that was a little alarming.

I guess there had been a lake here a long time ago (in Racetrack Basin, I heard), but it had dried up so many years ago, no one knew for sure when. We were in the middle of a decades-long drought and hardly ever saw rain. And certainly not enough rain to fill an entire basin.

"You need diapers, Gus?" asked Mayor Handsome, appearing from the back room. He put down his bucket of ostrich feed. You wouldn't expect to find an ostrich farm in the middle of the desert, but here it was, right in back of the Nowhere Market and Ostrich Farm. For five dollars, tourists could pet and feed the ostriches. It was a good thing Mayor Handsome didn't depend on tourists to feed his ostriches, though, because they'd have starved to death years ago.

Mayor Handsome was definitely the most successful person in Nowhere. Not only did he own the Nowhere Market and Ostrich Farm, he was also the mayor, apparently. At least, I thought he was. Everyone called him Mayor Handsome, but I suppose Mayor could have been his first name. Did a town the size of Nowhere really need a mayor? I didn't think there was ever any election. I seriously doubted Mayor Handsome's last name was Handsome, though. And if it was, why couldn't we call him Mr. Handsome? He insisted we always refer to him as Mayor Handsome. Like I said—weirdo. I had the sneaking suspicion he had given himself this name, though I found it entirely unsuitable.

He stood behind the counter, rubbing his beefy hands over his belly, which was seriously straining the buttons on his way-too-small cowboy shirt. I was always on full alert for one of those shirt buttons to burst off and come flying at my head. Then I would be forced to chop it midair like a ninja to protect myself. That would be awesome.

Mayor Handsome lifted one hand to the giant cowboy hat on top of his head and adjusted it. "Diapers?" he asked again with his strange accent—either Hungarian or Romanian or Slovakian. Or maybe Transylvanian. No one knew for sure where he had come from, and I guess no one cared. I doubted most of the population of Nowhere knew where Hungary or Romania or Slovakia were.

"No," I said. "Do you have any digging supplies?"

"*Vhat* digging supplies? Show-full?"

It took me a moment to figure out that a *show-full* was a shovel. I honestly had no idea what one would use to dig for gold in a mine on the verge of total death-inducing collapse. "Yeah."

Mayor Handsome led me to the shovel he had in the tool section. I picked it up and turned it over— twelve dollars. I put it back. "Do you have anything else? I only have seven dollars."

"Hand trowel is cheap." He pointed it out. "Only four dollars, but not good quality. Vhat you need it for?"

"Just a little, uh, gardening."

"Ground too hard. Handle vill break off. You have dee good soil at home?"

I shook my head and picked up a hammer and a chisel. "How about these?"

"Dat vould be strange vay to plant garden." He adjusted his large, boot-shaped, copper bolo tie. "But I let you have dose for only four dollars."

"I think I'll take them."

"Anyding else you need?" Mayor Handsome carried my stuff to the counter. "Diapers, corn remover?"

"No, I'm just going to get some snacks." I grabbed a box of Twinkies because nothing makes energy like pure sugar. All my grandma had at home was canned food and bologna. I'd definitely take some bologna when I got back, grateful I wouldn't be drinking it through a straw, thanks to Rossi.

I heard the door's bell jingle and saw Jessie Navarro enter the store. We nodded at each other in that cool sort of way. "Hey, Gus," he said casually.

"Hey, Jessie." Jessie and I had been good friends, best friends actually, up until last year. We didn't have a big fight or anything. I guess you could say we drifted apart in seventh grade when he started hanging out with the other Mexican kids who went to Nowhere

Elementary. They didn't tell me I couldn't hang out with them or anything; but when the people you're trying to be friends with constantly speak Spanish in front of you, and you don't understand Spanish, you start to feel a little insecure and left out. Plus, every time they laughed about something, I was sure it was about me. It didn't help that that they also pointed at me while laughing and sometimes said my name.

Now I hung out with this kid named Louis, who was actually really annoying, but it was better (and safer) than being a loser who ate lunch at a table alone. Even though Louis only talked about himself and his obsession with his creepy pet centipede. Even though Louis spit all over me when he talked about his pet centipede. He had some kind of salivation disorder. I knew I shouldn't look down on him for it—he obviously couldn't help it—but anyone would get tired of getting showered with pizza-flavored spittle on a regular basis. Yes, I've tasted it. I don't want to talk about it.

"Hey, Mayor Handsome, did you get those school supplies in for my pops?" Jessie asked.

"Oh, yeah. Is in dee back." Mayor Handsome left us standing at the counter alone together, then he peeked through the swinging doors that led to the back of the store. "Don't come back here."

Jessie and I both nodded. Everyone in Nowhere knew of Mayor Handsome's strict stay-away-from-the-back-of-my-store policy. There were a lot of theories floating around about what he was hiding back there: dead bodies (so predictable), drugs, gold, a giant collection of girlie teapots.

"You getting chicken pox?" Jessie took a step back.

I touched one of the spots on my face. "No, I had a meeting with a jumping cholla."

Jessie scowled. "I guess I don't have to ask who arranged that meeting."

"I guess not." I felt angry at Jessie—angry he no longer had to bear the brunt of Bo's torture. Ever since he had started hanging out with Ramiro's group, he was no longer one of Bo's targets. I guess I should have been glad for him, but I was only resentful at the moment. "Why weren't you at the races today?"

"I had better things to do." Jessie used to race up until about a year ago when he had a particularly bad crash and completely killed his dirt bike, but luckily not himself. It would take him forever to save up for another one. "If I can't be down there racing, I don't really have much interest in just standing there watching like some loser."

I cringed at his words. "Thanks," I mumbled.

"Oh, I didn't mean—"

"I know what you meant," I snapped.

Jessie cleared his throat. "What're you getting, Gus?" He picked up the hammer and chisel. "What's this for?"

I shrugged. "Nothing."

He threw them back on the counter with a loud clang. "Fine. Don't tell me."

I suddenly had the urge to tell someone, anyone, what I was about to do. What if I died? No one would know what had happened to me, and I knew Bo wouldn't tell anyone since he was the one who had sent me there.

"I'm going into the mine," I blurted out.

Jessie's head tilted back. "What mine?"

"Dead Frenchman," I said, much lower this time in case Mayor Handsome could hear us.

Jessie lifted the chisel. "I know we haven't been close this year, Gus, but I didn't think it would drive you to suicide."

I snatched the chisel from his hand. "I'm not suicidal. I have to go."

"Why?"

"Never mind."

"No, now you have to tell me."

"I made a deal with Bo Taylor. It's a long story, but he has Rossi's bike, and I can only get it back for her by going into the mine."

"Why is it your problem?"

"It just is." I was too embarrassed to tell him how Rossi had traded Loretta to save my life. Well, maybe not my life but at least my mouth. And possibly other essential body parts . . . intestines . . . certain holes.

Mayor Handsome returned and dropped a large paper bag on the counter. "Let's see. Vee have ten packs of markers," he said, rifling through the bag. "Glue sticks, pencils, paper, and five little scissors." He pronounced scissors like *skizzers*.

Jessie's dad taught first grade at Nowhere Elementary, and every year he could expect that most of the kids would show up with at least a few missing supplies. Some of the poorest kids showed up with none at all, and the Navarros spent their own money to buy the missing school supplies. Even though Jessie's mom also had a full-time job working at the scrapyard, I knew it was a big sacrifice for them.

Mayor Handsome pulled a couple of backpacks out of the bag. "And I put dese in for free for dee kids. For girl." He held up a pink backpack covered in poodles wearing tutus. Jessie and I glanced at each other. No kid at Nowhere Elementary, not even a first-grader, would be caught dead wearing that backpack. Because if they wore it, they would very likely end up dead. "And for boy." Mayor Handsome held up the other backpack, which was camouflage. That one was acceptable.

Mayor Handsome stuffed the backpacks into the large paper bag and pushed it across the counter to Jessie. "And you tell your pops I get a good discount and I only charge him cost for dese."

"Really?" Jessie said, hugging the bag to his chest.

"Of course. Is for dee kids." Mayor Handsome turned to me. "You ready to check out, Gus?"

"Yeah," I said. Jessie stood next to me, the giant bag of school stuff in his arms, while I paid for my pitiful supplies. I should have been buying a suit of armor, but I hadn't seen any on Mayor Handsome's shelves—not that I could have afforded one anyway had it been in stock.

"Hey, Mayor Handsome," I said as he handed me my bag, "what's gold worth? I mean, like a piece of gold. What's that worth?"

Mayor Handsome removed his oversize cowboy hat and scratched at his gray hair, somehow styled in a perfect slick wave despite the weight of the giant hat. "How much gold, Gus? Like a gold cow?"

What the . . . gold cow?

I shrugged. "I don't know, like a piece."

"Like a piece of gold toot?"

"Gold toot?" I asked.

"Gold toot." He tapped his giant, glaringly white front tooth.

"No." I shook my head. "I mean a regular little piece of gold. Like an ounce."

Mayor Handsome continued scratching at his head, and I hoped he didn't have lice. Someone always had lice in Nowhere, like this was their favorite place in the world to hang out. "I dink few hundred dollars."

"How big a piece would that be?" I said.

Mayor Handsome opened the cash register and pulled out a quarter. "Maybe like dis."

I nodded and smiled. "Great. So not too big then."

"Vhy you vant to know, Gus? You found some gold? Vhere you find it?" He slapped his beefy hands down on the counter.

"Just curious." I took a step back. "Thanks for your help." I waved to Mayor Handsome.

Jessie followed me out of the store, a look of concern on his face. I stopped on the front porch and turned to him. "How're your parents anyway?" I missed Jessie's family. They had always brought some sense of normalcy to this town—some sense of not everything in the world being so messed up all the time.

Jessie shrugged. "Okay, I guess. Busy."

"Busy with what?"

Jessie stared at me. "Why do you suddenly care about what's going on with me?"

"Am I not allowed to care?"

Jessie just stood there, his bushy eyebrows furrowed, his lips pursed.

I shook my head. "Fine. Later." I walked down the porch steps.

"You shouldn't go, Gus." I stopped and turned around. Jessie still stood on the porch. The giant bag of school supplies in his arms made him look small under the flickering porch light. "That mine's caved in all over the place."

The soft booms of the ostriches floated on the stuffy night air. "I told you. I don't have any choice."

"It's just a motorcyle," he said as I walked away.

But it was much more than that.

I SNUCK BACK INTO MY BEDROOM WINDOW

and laid my supplies out on the bed.

derisory: ridiculously small or inadequate

I tiptoed out of my room and stood at my grandma's door. She was snoring in her wet, hacking, gasping, choking way. I crept into the kitchen and made a couple of bologna sandwiches, filled a large pickle jar with water, took our only tiny flashlight out of the junk drawer, then headed back to my room. I should have bought extra batteries for the flashlight, but it was used so seldom, I hoped it would make it through the night. Plus, batteries were expensive. Plus, I completely hadn't thought about it.

Someone jumped out of my closet, and I shrieked in the most embarrassing way. Matthew Dufort threw himself onto my bed laughing.

My heart pounded. "You idiot," I gasped and opened my bedroom door, listening for my grandma's snoring. It still sounded like someone was gagging her to death in the next room, so I closed my door.

"Is this seriously what you're going to use to go into the mine?" Matthew tossed my small hammer down on the bed.

"It's all I've got." I pulled off my T-shirt and pitched it into my clothes hamper. I opened my dresser drawer and dug out my AT LEAST IT'S A DRY HEAT T-shirt with the neon pink cow skull on the front. My grandma had picked it up for herself at an old Western theme park several years ago and had given it to me when it grew a hole in the side. Thanks, Grandma. "What are you doing here anyway?"

"Bo sent me. He wants to make sure you don't go spray paint a rock or something."

Why hadn't *that* idea occurred to me? Well, it was too late now. "You're going to go into the mine with me?"

He shrugged. "Yeah. I'm your supervisor for the night."

"You always do what Bo orders you to do?"

He pushed his wavy, overgrown, light brown hair back from his eyes. The only way to get a haircut in Nowhere was to pay Mrs. Jenson ten dollars or cut your hair yourself. There wasn't much difference in the quality of the haircut, so most people cut their own hair. "It's better than eating cholla." He snickered.

I glared at him. "No, it's not."

His smile faded, and I suddenly remembered when Matthew and I were in second grade and he had naïvely handed out cheesy Valentine's Day cards to everyone. The one he'd given me had said *I'd be lion if I said you weren't sweet* and had a picture of a cartoon lion on it. He had been teased relentlessly for those cards, especially by Bo, who, even back then, was a bully.

I had found Matthew in the bathroom at lunchtime, crying in a stall. When he came out, I gave him my Valentine's card. Actually, I hadn't brought any Valentines because Grandma had spent the last of our money on a whole case of Spepper, and besides, the second grade kids were already too cynical for Valentine's cards. So I had made one from my notebook paper. I had written on it *I'd be lion if I said you weren't a great friend.* He'd wiped at his freckled cheeks and smiled at the card. "Do you mean it?" he'd said.

Matthew pushed me, and I fell onto my bed. "You

don't know what you're talking about, Gus. Anything's better than that."

I stared at him. "What kind of friend forces you to do things, especially things that could kill you?"

"Just shut up and get ready to go." He grabbed my backpack and threw it at me.

I emptied the Twinkies into my bag while Matthew scoffed again at the hammer and chisel. "You're never going to find anything with this stuff."

"Oh, do you have a jackhammer with you?"

"Do you even have a lantern?" He picked up the tiny flashlight. "How are you going to hold this and dig at the same time?"

I snatched the flashlight out of his hands. "I'll hold it in my mouth, I guess."

Matthew shook his head. "Well, at least you've got pickles. That will be a big help."

"It's water. Did you even bring water? You'll die of thirst before we ever get to the mine."

Matthew shrugged. "I'm like a camel."

"No, you're not." I snuck back into the kitchen and filled a jelly jar from the faucet. My grandma constantly saved old containers to store leftovers since we couldn't afford "that fancy plasticware stuff" as she always said with such disdain, like fancy plasticware was the reason we were so poor. We had so many old containers at this point, I wondered if she was planning on using old margarine and whipped topping tubs to battle zombies in the apocalypse.

I went back to my room, where Matthew was busy rummaging through my backpack. "Couldn't you at least have bought some Red Vines?" he said. "I hate Twinkies." I handed him the jelly jar. "Nice. Do you have any peanut butter to go with this?"

"Just be glad you have any water at all." I snatched my backpack away from him. "So stupid thinking you can walk five miles in the desert with no water," I mumbled as I slipped my backpack over my shoulders. "And there's no way I'll be sharing my snacks with you." I pointed my finger at him to make sure he knew I meant it. Plus, it made me feel tough.

"Hey, I'm not the reason we're heading there in the first place. That was your stupid idea, so be careful who you're calling stupid. Stupid." Matthew climbed out the window.

I looked around my room for a second, wondering if this was the last time I would ever see it. I was surprised to find it didn't make me feel sad at all. I felt . . . nothing about it. Nothing at all.

I climbed out the window and quietly closed it.

"How long do you think it will take us to get there?" Matthew asked.

"It's about two and a half miles to the other side of Hollow Mountain, so I'd say about forty-five minutes at most."

And so we headed out into the dark desert, the pickle jar of water sloshing around loudly in my backpack.

9:00 PM

LUCKILY, THE MOON WAS FULL, SO I COULD

watch my steps as I walked without turning on the flashlight and wasting the battery life. I scanned the ground for rattlesnakes. I once heard the majority of people bitten by rattlesnakes were drunk men at night, and I believed it because it had happened to my own great-grandfather. I was two for three here. And no, I wasn't drunk.

I could see the mine in the distance as we got closer—a dark hole in the middle of the silvery mountain.

abyss: a deep or seemingly endless chasm

"You should just give this up, and we can both go home," Matthew said. "Forget about Rossi. Bo will never give that bike back anyway. He's determined to win tomorrow."

"Yeah. And he knows the only way he can win is for her not to race."

I stood at the entrance of the mine and took a swig of my warm water, which did have a faint pickle flavor. I evaluated the blackness. Yeah, it was really black. Evaluation over.

I turned on the flashlight and inched forward, Matthew following closely behind. "Maybe you shouldn't follow me," I said. The guy was a jerk for being friends with Bo, but if the mine did cave in, I didn't want him to die, too.

"I have to make sure you find the gold in the actual mine."

"Oh yeah, I forgot. Bo's orders."

Matthew shoved me forward. "Stop being a baby and move."

Someone had already smashed several slats in the wooden barricade, so we easily climbed through them. The mine smelled all of its one hundred years old—like dirt and rot and hot air that never moved. I shined the flashlight on the large wooden planks that were somehow holding the mountain up above us. *Please don't fail*, I begged the century-old wood, imagining the entire mountain coming down on our heads. We *might* not make it out if that happened.

"We'd better go in deep," Matthew said. "I'm sure this whole area is cleaned out."

"I don't need your advice." I didn't want to go deeper into the mine, but I knew Matthew was right. I pointed the flashlight ahead as we walked slowly together. The air was so hot and thick, I could feel it pushing back on me with every step. I was aware of each breath as it filled my lungs, making them heavy.

"That's the part that caved in when those two drunk guys went in," Matthew whispered when we came to a fork. One direction was a mess of rubble. "I guess they're still in there."

"No. They found those bodies. But the dead Frenchman is still back there somewhere."

"Creepy. I saw this ghost hunting show, and Dead Frenchman Mine was on it. They said it was haunted by all the people who've died in here."

"That's ridiculous, Matthew." I'd seen the show, too. Everyone in Nowhere had seen it. It wasn't often Nowhere got in the news or on TV, but when it did, everyone watched.

"They had this machine that could record what the

ghosts said," Matthew went on. "And they recorded one saying, 'Snooze snout toe duty.'"

"What does that even mean?"

Matthew shrugged. "I don't know, but they said it was proof there were ghosts in here. One of the guys on the show also got scratched by the ghosts. He showed the scratches on his arm."

I rolled my eyes. "Or maybe he bumped into the rocky wall."

"No way. These were definitely ghost scratches."

We went down a different corridor until we reached a dead end. "I guess we can try here." I shined the flashlight on the dirt wall embedded with rock. "It's as good a place as any."

I eased my backpack onto the ground, careful not to break my jar of water, and removed the hammer and chisel. Then I put it back on in case I needed to make a quick escape. I tapped on the wall gently with my chisel.

"That's going to do a lot," Matthew said.

"I'm testing it," I snapped. Truth was, I had no idea what I was doing, but I was terrified the whole mine would cave in if I hit the wall any harder.

I built up my courage with every tap and eventually

was pounding the chisel hard enough to take some chunks out of the wall. "Why don't you inspect the pieces I get off and see if you find any gold?" I told Matthew, who was holding the flashlight for me.

"Can't do that and hold the flashlight and jelly jar at the same time."

"You *could* put the jelly jar down."

"A bug might crawl on it."

I shook my head and went back to hammering the chisel. And then I heard something. I stopped, thinking it might have been an echo. "Did you hear that?" I said.

"Hear what? I don't hear any—"

"Shh!" I stared at the ground and concentrated on listening. I definitely heard something—voices.

I looked up at Matthew. "Oh. My. Gosh," he said, the flashlight shaking in his hands. His eyes bulged with fear. "It's the ghosts!"

10:00 PM

MATTHEW DROPPED THE JELLY JAR OF
water, and it shattered on the ground at his feet. My
heart beat rapidly. I knew in my brain ghosts weren't
real. But, you know, sometimes brains malfunction.

I grabbed at the flashlight. "Turn it off!" I whis-
per-shrieked, but both Matthew's and my hands were
shaking. We fumbled it for a full five seconds or so
before finally getting it off.

Now it was totally dark. I could barely hear over
Matthew's hyperventilating, and maybe my own. We
heard voices again. Matthew grabbed on to me. Maybe
I grabbed on to him, too. No one ever needs to know
about that, though.

"They're getting closer," Matthew said. They were
definitely getting closer. "What do we do?"

Then we heard a voice shout, "Gus!"

Matthew squeezed me. "It knows your name! It's here for you!"

My brain was starting to think clearly again. "Shut up."

I heard her voice again. "Gus!" Rossi shouted. "Where are you?"

"Back here," I called.

"Don't tell it where we are!" Matthew cried.

"It's Rossi." I shoved Matthew off of me.

A small dim light traveled toward us, and Rossi and Jessie came into view. I walked to them. "What are you guys doing here?"

Rossi held a lantern up in one hand, her helmet in the other. "Jessie told me what you were up to."

I frowned at him. "Why? Why'd you do that, man?"

"She should know you were planning on killing yourself for her."

"As you can see, we're totally fine."

"We?" Jessie said.

I turned and pointed into the dark. "Matthew's cowering back there somewhere, probably changing his pants. He thought you guys were ghosts."

"Shut up, Gus," Matthew shouted. "So did you."

Rossi looked at me in the dim light. "I'm grateful for what you're doing, Gus, but it's not worth it."

"I'm doing this no matter what."

"Gus," Rossi pleaded.

I crossed my arms. "I'm not leaving."

"There's no gold in here, Gus," Jessie said.

"I guess I'll find out." I turned to Rossi. "Why did you bring your helmet?"

She rapped on it with her knuckles. "Protection." She lifted it and put it over her head, her long pony-tail flowing out the back. Then she swung her backpack around and pulled out an icepick. "If you're not leaving, then I'm helping. It's my bike, after all." She glanced around the mine for a moment and sighed. "Dead Frenchman Mine, huh? Leave it to some European dude to wreck a perfectly good mountain that didn't belong to him." She slammed her pick into the wall.

When Matthew saw Rossi chipping away at the wall, the helmet on her head, he groaned. "Why didn't I bring *my* helmet? I can't believe I have to stand here and watch you losers dig with tiny hammers and . . . sword-like thingies."

"*Pendejo*," Jessie muttered as he turned the lantern up.

I snorted; I may not have spoken Spanish fluently, but I knew what *that* word meant. And no, it doesn't mean *you're an awesome human being* or *thank you for blessing us with your presence.*

"What did you say?" Matthew asked.

Jessie took a screwdriver out of Rossi's bag and shrugged. "I said, 'Hey, let's dig . . . oh.'"

Matthew eyed Jessie with suspicion. "I don't think that's what you said."

"I don't care what you think."

Matthew leaned against the wall and yawned, his arms crossed. "This is the most pitiful bunch of digging tools I've ever seen." He really did look like our supervisor.

"Why don't you get off your lazy butt and help us?" Jessie said.

"I don't have anything to dig with."

"I bet you could find a sharp rock," Jessie said. "I mean, besides the one on top of your neck."

Matthew glanced at the ground. "None around. And why would I want to help anyway?"

"Because you're not such a bad guy," Rossi said through her helmet opening. "I don't think you're as mean as you've led people to believe."

"Of course I am. I'm totally . . ."

"Menacing," I finished for him. "You're terrifying. Horrible. You give us all nightmares." I felt a slap on the back of my head. "Ow!" I shouted and turned around.

Matthew glared at me. "Stop talking and keep digging."

Jessie stopped scraping at the wall with the screwdriver and glared at Matthew. "Aren't you related to that dead French guy?"

Matthew scoffed at Jessie's comment. "Where'd you hear that?"

"William *Dufort*," Jessie said. "That was the guy's name. Like yours."

"Doesn't mean we're related." Matthew shifted from foot to foot.

I stopped digging and looked at him. "What are the odds that two different families by the name of Dufort would end up in a town like Nowhere?"

Matthew shrugged. "I'm not a philosopher so I have no idea." I wasn't sure Matthew knew what a philosopher was.

Jessie continued glaring at Matthew. "Why don't you just admit that you're related to that jerk?"

Matthew glared back at Jessie. "What do you care?"

Jessie threw his screwdriver down, and it bounced on the hard dirt ground. "Because he killed my great-grandfather and stole his gold." Jessie stepped forward and shoved Matthew.

Matthew pushed Jessie back. "Get off me, man. Last I heard, your great-grandpa is the one who stole the gold and shot *him*."

They continued bickering and pushing each other. I looked at Rossi. She had stopped chipping at the wall and was watching them through her helmet opening. She removed it and tilted her head to the side a little bit. "What's this all about?"

They stopped arguing and looked at her. "What? You don't know the story?" Jessie asked her.

Rossi shook her head.

"I thought everyone in Nowhere knew the history of Dead Frenchman Mine," Matthew said.

"She hasn't lived here very long," I said. "She probably hasn't heard about it."

"Let me fill you in, Rossi," Jessie snarled, shooting evil looks at Matthew. "That guy's"—Jessie pointed dramatically at Matthew—"great-grandfather and my great-grandfather were partners. They mined a whole bag of gold out of this place. They were supposed to split it fifty-fifty, but his great-grandfather was a lying, cheating, backstabbing, murdering piece of garbage who stole the gold and shot his partner."

"That's a lie!" Matthew shouted. "Your great-grand-father is the one who stole the gold and shot *him*. My dad told me the whole story."

Jessie smirked. "You mean before he ditched your sorry butt?"

That did it—Matthew lunged at Jessie, and then the two of them were rolling around in the dirt together.

I stood there, no clue what to do, kind of wishing they'd stop, but also enjoying watching Jessie push Matthew's face into the dirt. The flashlight flew out of Matthew's hand and rolled toward me. I picked it up and pointed it at them to get a better view.

"Stop it!" Rossi screamed. "Are you two really going to fight in a mine that could cave in on you at any moment?"

They seemed to come to their senses and pushed off of one another. They stood up, breathing heavily, keeping their eyes on each other in case the other tried to pull something.

"This has nothing to do with you now," Rossi said. "It was a long time ago. Maybe you're not even related to those men."

"It has everything to do with me," Jessie snapped. "I know that guy was my great-grandfather. Every-one in my family knows it. And maybe if some lowlife hadn't killed him and stolen everything he had, then my great-grandma wouldn't have been left high and dry with a baby to care for. Maybe we wouldn't still be here, poor as dogs, not even enough money to get a new dirt bike, living on scraps. *Literally.*" Jessie picked his screwdriver back up and slammed it into the wall.

"I hope you're pleased with yourself," I said to Matthew and turned back to the wall.

"What did I do?" Matthew said. "He started it."

I continued chipping away at the wall with my hammer and chisel. Those guys could fight all night long if they wanted, but I was going to focus on the work at hand.

I pounded on the chisel, which barely went in a millimeter with each hit, trying to find the spots in the wall that weren't filled with rock. I guess I had gotten over my fear of the mine caving in already because I was hitting it as hard as I could. The mine echoed with the sounds of our pounding away, when suddenly my chisel went all the way into the wall.

I stood back, not sure what to make of it. "What . . ."

Rossi stopped and stared at my chisel. "How'd you do that?"

"With one hit."

"Stop showing off, Gus," Jessie said. I ignored him

and grabbed the screwdriver out of his hand. "Hey," he protested.

I held the screwdriver up to the wall next to the chisel and pounded it with my hammer while the others watched. After a few whacks, it, too, went all the way into the wall. "It's like . . . there's nothing back there," I said.

"That's freaky," said Jessie. "Maybe we should dig somewhere else."

"Maybe it's a hidden corridor," I said.

Rossi reached up a slender finger and touched the screwdriver. "Nothing," she whispered. "Do you think. . . "

"Think what?" I asked.

She looked at me. "Do you think the mountain really is hollow?"

Jessie laughed behind me.

Her brown eyes were barely visible in the lantern light. "Why would they call it that?" she said.

I looked at the chisel embedded in the wall. "I always thought it was because of all the mines."

Rossi gripped the handle of the screwdriver and pulled it out in one quick motion. A whistling sound came from the small hole. She stuck the screwdriver back in and made twisting motions, causing the whistling to grow louder as the hole enlarged. "Hand me your flashlight." I gave it to her. She held it up to the hole and peered through. Air streamed out, blowing Rossi's loose strands of hair back from her face.

"Maybe you shouldn't do that, Rossi," I said. "What if it's all filled with methane gas?" She ignored me as she stared into the hole. "What do you see?" I whispered, suddenly terrified, like we were on the brink of opening some portal to who-knows-where, but knowing Nowhere, it would be somewhere extremely not good.

Rossi swallowed. "Nothing."

I heard a splitting sound, and my heart jumped in my chest. All four of us looked up at the rotten plank responsible for keeping the mountain from coming down on us. *You're not doing your job!* I wanted to scream at it.

Instead, I managed to get the word *run* out, but apparently not loud enough because the others still stood there, frozen.

"Run!" I managed to shout this time.

I turned and ran in the direction we had come in, following the others. We barely made it ten feet when the mine started crumbling right over our heads.

SO WHAT DOES ONE DO WHEN A MINE

starts to cave in on them? Well, if you're thirteen years old, apparently you crouch in a corner, cover your head, and cry. Not necessarily in that order.

We huddled together as the mountain rumbled and collapsed. I watched helplessly as a piece of beam came down on Rossi. Fortunately, she had managed to get her helmet on again—I guess it had been a good idea to bring it after all.

When the rumbling finally quieted, I coughed the dust out of my lungs. It was hard to breathe in the thick air, but I managed to choke out, "Are you okay?"

"Okay," Jessie croaked next to me.

"Okay," Matthew said.

Rossi pointed the little flashlight at her face. "Okay," she said from under her helmet.

I took the flashlight from her and shined it around us—we were surrounded by rubble. I was reminded of Louis, the kid with the pet centipede and salivation disorder. Louis's trailer was so filled with junk, you had to walk through tunnels to get from room to room. I always felt suffocated when I was in his trailer because no matter where I stood, I was closed in by stuff. The mine was like that right now, only there were no tunnels, just walls.

claustrophobia: extreme fear of confined
places

I looked above me and saw what had saved our lives—a giant boulder jutted out overhead and had prevented the mine from caving in right over us.

The air was thick with dust—almost too thick to breathe—and we all coughed and gasped.

Jessie sniffled beside me. "What are we going to do? No one even knows we're here." I shined the light on him and Matthew and saw they were holding each other in what could almost be considered a romantic embrace.

Matthew pushed Jessie off of him in disgust. "We're trapped," Matthew said. "We're trapped and we're going to die. We're going to die horrible agonizing deaths. We'll suffocate. Or we'll starve to death."

"No." Jessie sneezed. "We'll die of thirst before we starve to death."

"Stop it," I told them.

Rossi looked at the rubble surrounding us, breathing heavily. "I think we can crawl over it."

The thought of trying to squeeze between the rubble and the new ceiling of the mine wasn't appealing. But neither was sitting here, waiting to die.

"Remember that wall?" Rossi said. "The one your chisel went through?"

"Yeah."

"Maybe it's another corridor. Maybe we can get back there—it's only about ten feet away. Maybe we can break through the wall."

"And maybe we'll die in the rubble," said Matthew.

"Maybe," said Rossi.

"Or maybe it's filled with menthol," said Jessie.

"Methane," I said.

Jessie threw up his arms. "Oh, like that's any better."

"Maybe to all those things," said Rossi. "But sitting here doing nothing is not an option."

"Easy for you to say," said Jessie. "You have a helmet."

Rossi lifted the helmet off her head and took a deep breath of dirty air. "Here." She handed it to Jessie. "You can wear it."

Jessie's eyes were huge as he quickly pushed the helmet over his frazzled hair, which was more gray than dark brown right now.

Matthew shook his head. "Wimp."

"I'll go first," I said.

Jessie nodded, the helmet flopping forward. "Great idea."

I rolled my eyes. "I'm the smallest. If I can't fit, then none of you can, either."

Rossi stared at me. She was breathing hard and her forehead was covered in sweat. "I lost my backpack. Our water was in it."

"Don't worry," I told her. "I have a jar of water." One jar of water for four people.

I realized immediately I wasn't going to be able to hold my flashlight and scale the rubble—a mix of rocks and earth and rotten planks—at the same time. I stuck it in my mouth and started to climb the unstable pile.

My hands slipped and I tumbled back down, along with a bunch of rocks that banged up my legs. "Okay," I muttered. "Again."

I grabbed at a different place in the debris and once more attempted to climb the rubble. It was a one step forward, one step backward sort of process as I fell back down. "I don't know if I can get up there."

"I'll help you," Rossi said. She moved the lantern closer to the pile.

"Good thing I grabbed the lantern," said Jessie, clearly proud of his bravery.

"You were already holding it when the mine caved in," Matthew said. "There was no grabbing involved."

I groaned. Scaling the rubble was starting to seem like fun compared to sitting with these two. Rossi held out two hands linked together, and I stepped into them. Then she hoisted me up. I grabbed onto the rocks and planks with all my might, the sharp edges tearing at my thin T-shirt and the skin beneath. When I started to slide back down again, Rossi pushed at my butt to keep me up.

Seriously, here I was in a collapsed mine, trying to scale a mountain of rubble, hoping to break through a wall to who-knows-where, likely to die at any moment, and all I could think was *Rossi Scott is touching my butt*.

After what felt like an eternity, I made it to where the rubble wasn't so loose and steep and was able to pull myself on top of the pile. I lay there for a moment, trying to catch my breath. The ceiling was barely above my head. I was sandwiched. I felt the panic rising in my chest and did my best to squash it back down.

I aimed the flashlight ahead of me—I could probably squeeze forward over the pile, but I couldn't make out the far wall. All I saw in that direction was blackness. Nothing. I turned my head to call to Rossi, "I think we can make it."

I inched forward over the painful rubble. The sharp rocks dug into every part of me. I was glad I had worn the AT LEAST IT'S A DRY HEAT T-shirt instead of one of my good ones from Dollar General in Casa Grande. I didn't often go to Casa Grande, and a new pack of T-shirts was a luxury in my life.

I heard a lot of grunting behind me as the rest of them tried to push one another up the rubble. All three of them were larger and stronger than I was, so it didn't take nearly as long.

I could barely breathe as rocks pushed into my diaphragm. The air was so thick with dust, I was amazed I hadn't suffocated already. I came to a section that was too tight to squeeze through, so I worked on moving rocks and earth away while I waited for the others. "It's really tight right here."

Matthew crawled up beside me and helped to clear more inches. That's all we were squeezing through— inches of space. "My life doesn't seem so bad right now," Matthew said as he moved a jagged rock to the side. "I don't want it to be over already."

I took a deep breath of gravy-thick air and swallowed the dirt in my throat. "It won't be."

I SLID DOWN THE RUBBLE, LANDING ON

the hard ground with a jolt. My clothes were torn everywhere and covered in blood from the many scrapes and scratches. I watched the others as they skidded down—they were as ragged as I was.

"Is everyone okay?" I asked them as they stood and faced the opening in the wall.

Jessie removed the helmet. "I think so. My whole body is burning. And every inch of me is sore. My head is throbbing. And my lungs feel like they're filled with cement. I think I might actually die. But I'm okay."

Jessie hadn't yet been hardened by life like the rest of us. He was too soft.

I turned to Rossi. "Okay?"

She nodded slowly. She didn't speak as she grabbed

the helmet and lantern from Jessie, stepped forward, and climbed through the opening in the wall, which had collapsed along with the mine.

I looked at the two guys and shrugged. "I guess we're going."

"No time to waste, huh, Rossi?" Jessie called. "Like, no time to make sure there's not menthol, or some kind of, I don't know, buried monster waiting on the other side. I once saw this movie, and they uncovered a dragon in this mine, and . . ."

I ignored Jessie as he rambled on. I opened my backpack and quickly checked my supplies—the Twinkies were a little flattened, but the pickle jar was still intact. I pulled out my pocket watch and flipped it open. It hadn't been damaged, other than the backing still being a bit loose, and I saw it was just after midnight. I put the watch back in my pocket, shined the flashlight ahead of me, and stepped through the dark opening after Rossi.

"Would you please shut up?" Matthew yelled at Jessie as he nervously droned on about monsters and dragons and deadly ancient microbes. I was pretty sure none of those were in this hole. *Pretty* sure.

"You guys should stick close together," I told them. "You know, since you don't have a light." They grumbled as they followed me. We seemed to be in some kind of large tunnel.

"There's a larger opening this way," Rossi called back to us.

I watched my steps carefully as I followed her. The ground was nothing but rocks, making it difficult to walk without my ankles twisting. I stopped for a moment and aimed the flashlight at the rocky walls—this didn't seem like part of the mine. It didn't appear man-made at all. I looked ahead and didn't see Rossi anymore. "Rossi?" My voice echoed off the rock walls.

"I'm in here." She sounded far away.

We followed her voice, stumbling over the rocky ground, until we found ourselves in a gigantic room. Rossi turned the lantern up as high as it would go.

"What is this place?" Matthew said. "I've never seen anything like it."

I gazed around at the many spires and spikes jutting up from the floor, the ceiling that was melting down over us. "A cave," I whispered.

"This place is creepy." Jessie pointed to the tip of a spire. "What are these things?"

"Stalagmites," I said. "Or stalagtites. I can't remember."

"Stalag*mites* grow up from the ground." Rossi held the lantern up. "Stala*ctites* grow down from the ceiling." We all looked at her. The sudden silence between us caused a buzzing in my ears. I didn't know silence like that existed. "What?" she finally said, and the terrible buzzing stopped. "I read it in a magazine once."

Matthew eyed her suspiciously. "What magazine? *National Nerdographic*?"

I squatted down so I could more closely inspect one of the stalagmites. "You know what this place reminds me of? That ride in Disneyland—Thunder Mountain. It drives through a cave like this. Of course that cave is all fake."

Everyone was staring at me now. "You've been to Disneyland?" Matthew asked like I told them I had gone to Mars. "What's it like?"

"Uh." I didn't like to talk about it. I didn't even like to *think* about it. Why had I brought it up in the first place? "It was okay."

Jessie glanced at me. He knew why I didn't want to talk about it. And I knew he wouldn't betray my secrets, no matter what had gone on between us over the last year.

"When did you go?" Matthew said.

"I was, uh, six. Before I moved here." Actually, it was the same day. I tried to change the subject. "At least it's not too hot in here. It's cooler than outside."

"A lot cooler," Matthew said as we walked slowly through the cave over the crumbled rock floor, being careful not to trip and fall on a stalagmite.

impale: pierce or transfix with a sharp
   instrument

I resisted the urge to kick one of the stupid stalagmites. "I guess we won't be finding any gold now," I grumbled.

"That was a long shot anyway, Gus," Jessie said. "I'd be pretty happy if we just, like, don't die at this point."

"But what about Rossi's bike?" I said.

"I agree with Jessie," Rossi said. "We should just focus on getting out of here. If there even is a way out of here."

I took in a deep breath. "What if there's not?"

They all stopped and looked at me, six huge eyes. "Let's just assume that there is," Rossi finally said. "There *has* to be," she said a bit more firmly.

"When we get out we'll have to go back to the mine and search more," I said.

"Are you crazy?" Jessie said. "I wouldn't go back in that mine for a million dollars."

"Me neither," Matthew agreed.

I looked at Rossi. "We can figure out another way, Gus," she said. "No one's going back in that mine. Including you."

I moped as we walked in silence for a while, maneuvering around boulders and cracks in the ground and stalagmites until Jessie covered his nose and said, "Geez, what is that?"

I sniffed the air. Something was starting to smell.

"What *is* that?" Jessie said again. "It smells like our kitty litter box if we didn't change it for a year. And it was covered in rotten potatoes. And burnt hair. And barf."

"It's pretty bad," Matthew said.

I looked down and saw that I was standing in some kind of weird dirt—clumps of dark brown rice that disintegrated into powder like used charcoal as I stepped on it.

"Gross." Jessie lifted his shoe and shook it, the dirt turning into a small dust cloud around his foot.

We moved on, but the mounds of strange dirt continued to get bigger until our shoes were completely submerged. "What is this stuff?" Matthew said. "I think it's what smells."

I bent down and inspected it—the pieces were oval-shaped. We'd had plenty of mice in our trailer, and this looked similar to the nice presents they left behind in my underwear drawer. "It's some kind of poop, I think." My grandma probably would have been interested in it.

Rossi slowly raised the lantern above her and tilted her head back. "It is."

We all looked up. There were hundreds, maybe thousands, of bats hanging from the ceiling above us.

The lantern shook in Rossi's hand. "It's bat guano."

"What's guano?" Matthew asked.

"Why you guano know?" I laughed nervously at my own bad joke. No one laughed with me. "It's poop."

Jessie let out a pitiful whimper. "This isn't happening."

"No, no. It's good," I said. "They have to go in and out, right? To eat, I mean. There must be a way out of the cave."

Rossi looked at me. "Right."

"We'll keep going. I'm sure they won't notice us," I said.

"Right," Rossi said again.

"Are they vampire bats?" Matthew asked. "Or are they, like, the fruity kind?"

"They're vampire bats, for sure," I said. "Don't wake them up or they'll suck you dry."

"Shut up, Gus," Matthew and Jessie both said.

"I'm kidding. They probably just eat bugs. Or fruities."

"Do they have rabies?" Matthew asked.

"How should I know?" I said. "I'm not a philosopher."

Jessie snorted. "Good one."

"Are you guys making fun of me?" said Matthew.

"You just give us so much to work with," said Jessie.

And then, to my horror, Matthew picked up a handful of the bat poop and threw it at Jessie. It hit him in the chest and exploded, forming a poufy poop cloud that sparkled in the light of my flashlight. Some of it drifted to me and landed on my arm. I aimed the flashlight at it—it was filled with insect wings. I guess the bats weren't the fruity kind after all.

"Don't!" I ordered them, wiping the wings off my arms. But there was no way Jessie wasn't going to retaliate.

I saw that Rossi was already heading back the way we had come in, trudging through the bat poop as quickly as she dared. She obviously knew what was coming.

shenanigans: silly or high-spirited behavior; mischief

Jessie threw a handful of bat poop right in Matthew's face, creating another glittering poop cloud. It was kind of beautiful in a revolting sort of way. Matthew coughed, and I hoped the poop dust wouldn't make them sick. Then again, Nowhere's kids' lungs were accustomed to all kinds of contaminants—seasoned by a lifetime of harsh desert dust and indoor smoking.

A bat swooped over my head. "Stop disturbing the bats!" I commanded. But they were in a full-blown poop fight now—coughing and sneezing inside a giant glistening poopy dust cloud.

More and more bats were waking up from the ceiling and flying around the cave. I walked as quickly as I could in Rossi's direction, careful not to trip into the repulsive piles.

I turned around just in time to see Matthew take a large handful of poop and smear it right on top of Jessie's head, rubbing it in with great enthusiasm. Jessie tackled him to the ground. For the second time that night. Then they were rolling around in the poop together.

I turned away from their ridiculous fight. And then I watched as a bat swooped down and landed in Rossi's hair.

Rossi was pretty cool. She was one of the best racers in Nowhere. She seemed strong and tough. But right now, as the bat fluttered its wings, further entangling itself in her long dark hair, she was just a thirteen-year-old girl with a bat in her hair.

She dropped the lantern and helmet right into a large pile of bat guano and let out the loudest, highest-pitched scream I'd ever heard. I ran to her, kicking up a poop dust devil as I went. "Calm down," I said, but she was completely panicked, screaming and turning in circles, slapping at her head. "Calm down!"

She finally stopped, her chest heaving, her eyes slammed shut. "Get it out, get it out, get it out."

I didn't want to touch the bat, but I had no choice. I carefully untangled her hair from around it while it flapped wildly. I resisted the instinct to pull my hand away every time its wings grazed my fingers. "It's always best to remove it quickly when you don't expect it," I said, but she didn't smile. She didn't seem to hear me at all. I finally got enough hair loose, and the bat flew away.

Rossi's chest was still heaving as she smoothed her frazzled hair with one trembling hand and picked up her helmet with the other. "Thank you, Gus." I could tell she was trying to be casual as she brushed the poop off her helmet. "That was quite brave of you."

"You're welcome." I didn't tell her she had bat poop on her shoulder. I picked up the lantern, brushed the poop off it as well as I could, and handed it to her.

The bats were flying all around us. "Are you finished now?" I asked Jessie and Matthew. Both of them were covered head to toe in the poop. At least it wasn't sludgy, so they mostly looked like they had been diving in powder.

They nodded. I pointed my flashlight in the direction we had come from. "Maybe we should try the other way."

"Why?" Matthew asked.

"Because that's the direction the bats are flying." Rossi's voice was raspier than usual—probably from the dust and screaming. "There must be a way out down there."

The other way was an obstacle course of large boulders and narrow, rocky tunnels. At one point, the ceiling got so low (or the floor got so high), we had to crawl through on our hands and knees, bellies low to the ground.

I crouched down and took deep breaths of cool cave air while I crawled through the tight space. If anyone had ever asked me what rock smelled like, I probably would have said nothing. But now I knew that rock had a smell—and it was the smell of this cave.

Rossi was mumbling something. I strained to listen. "Three minutes, three days, three weeks," she was saying, her voice trembling. "Three minutes, three days, three weeks."

"What are you talking about?" I asked her.

"The rule of three," she said, breathing heavily. "You can survive three minutes without air, three days without water, and three weeks without food."

"Why are you thinking about that?" Jessie cried. "Knock it off!"

"We have air." I breathed in. "We have water." Yeah, one glass jar of pickle water. "And we have food, too." Or at least stuff that barely qualified as food. "And besides, that rule sounds pretty flexible. I mean, if we were outside in the middle of the day, we couldn't go even three hours without water, so I'm sure we can go longer than three days in here in the cool dark."

"How long can you survive without light?" Matthew asked.

"That's a stupid question," Jessie said. "We're not plants. It's not like we need to photo . . . graphisize or whatever."

"That's not what I meant," Matthew snapped. "How long will these batteries last?"

I stopped crawling. If we lost the light, nothing else would matter. "Maybe we should only use one light at a time to conserve batteries," I said. I didn't wait for them to respond as I flipped off the flashlight. The intense quiet caused that horrible buzzing in my ears again. We moved on, the lantern our only light now.

"I hope no one here is closet-tropic," Matthew said.

I stopped and turned my head to Matthew. "Closet-tropic?"

Jessie laughed. "Oh man. He means cluster-phobic. What a moron."

"Shut up, Jessie," Matthew said. "You don't even know what I'm talking about."

"The word is *claustrophobic*," Rossi said. "And, please, let's not discuss it."

"Why, Rossi?" I asked. "You're not closet-tropic are you?"

"No . . . I . . . just don't . . . like . . . small spaces."

"I believe that makes you closet-tropic," I said.

"Making jokes . . . doesn't help," she breathed.

"And it's not funny, either," Matthew said. "Who cares what the word is anyway? You guys are a bunch of book nerds."

"I'm no book nerd," Jessie said. "Gus on the other hand . . ."

I gave Jessie a warning look and mouthed, "Don't."

"What about Gus?" Matthew asked.

"Nothing," Jessie said. "Mind your own business, Matthew."

"You're the one who brought it up, Jesus." Matthew took extra care to loudly and slowly pronounce Jessie's real name *gee-zus*, like the guy from the Bible, when it's really pronounced *hay-soos*, like a bale of hay and Dr. Seuss.

"That's not how you say my name, Matthew. It's pronounced *hay-soos*."

Matthew grunted as he pushed himself through a particularly narrow space. "Whatever."

"I wish you guys would just shut up and crawl." I hadn't meant it to sound so mean. Okay, yes, I did. Those two were getting on my nerves.

"Don't tell us what to do, Fer-gus." Jessie drew out the *Fer* part of my name like *Ferrrrrrrr*.

"Oh man," Matthew said. "Fergus? That's such a dweeb name."

Rossi stopped and looked at me. "Fergus? It's Irish, right?"

I shrugged. "I don't know."

Rossi wiped sweat from her forehead and took a deep breath. She started moving forward again. "Well, it sounds Irish."

"What do you know about what sounds Irish, you weirdo?" Matthew said. "It could be Chinese."

"Or Viking," Jessie added, then did his silly, heaving laugh that always cracked me up.

"Viking," I said quietly to myself. *Yeah, I liked that.*

"I'm fairly certain it's not Chinese," Rossi said. "Or Viking."

"Who asked you anyway, whatever-your-name-is?" Matthew said.

I stopped. "What do you mean?"

"Oh yeah," Matthew said. "Like she just happens to have the same name as one of the greatest motorcycle riders of all time. Yeah, right."

Sweat dripped down Rossi's strained face. "Isn't it your real name?" I asked her.

She didn't answer me—just stared straight ahead and moved forward like a crab, pushing the helmet ahead of her as she went.

I turned to Matthew. "I really wish you would shut up."

"Why are you getting mad at me? She's the one you can't trust."

I gritted my teeth. "You've been listening to Bo too much."

"Oh, really? Ask her where she got her gear from. Or how she keeps up her bike. Go ahead."

"I don't need to ask her anything."

"You know it costs money to do that. It's not like her dad is rich. She doesn't work. There's only one option left."

I tried to ignore him as I periodically glanced at Rossi, but she was totally expressionless.

"She's a thief," Matthew said.

"Shut up." I could feel the anger, the need to defend her, rising inside me like it had earlier that day. That hadn't ended well, and I definitely didn't need to get into a fistfight in such a cramped space. Then again, with my small size, that might actually work in my favor. "How do *you* get *your* motorcycle parts?"

"I do stuff for Bud at his shop, and he helps me work on my bike in return. And Bo told me that Rossi—"

I cut Matthew off. "When will you get it through your head that everything that guy says is a lie?"

"Whatever. But he's not the only liar around."

Rossi just quietly shook her head. The look on her face told me Matthew's words weren't even worth a response from her.

"What's your point anyway?" I said. "Trying to get everyone mad?"

"No. Just that I'm the only one here who isn't pretending to be something they're not."

"Yeah right," Jessie and I both said at the same time.

"What's that supposed to mean?"

Finally Rossi spoke. "You pretend to be a mean bully who likes Bo."

"To protect yourself," I added. "You know it's true."

Matthew didn't seem to have a comeback to that.

THE TIGHT SPACE FINALLY OPENED UP, AND

we were able to stand. Rossi held the lantern out. "Looks like we can walk a little easier now," I said.

I didn't know if everyone was mad or completely worn out from the mine, the bats, and our crawl through the rock, but we were all quiet. Rossi walked in front of us with the lantern, and I tried to keep my eyes on the ground so I didn't trip over the many grooves, cracks, bumps, and rocks, but the cave was just so interesting, I kept looking up. A nearby wall caught my eye. "Hey, you guys!" I said. "Look at this."

They gathered around to check out what I had discovered—drawings. But not regular drawings anyone could have done. These were old. *Really* old.

"They're petroglyphs," Rossi said, holding the lantern up to the wall.

Matthew rolled his eyes. "More *National Nerdographic* talk."

We all stood silently as we looked over the carvings that covered the rock wall. Some of them were clearly people—stick figures with their arms and legs up, some holding what looked like canes, some with ornaments on their heads. There were also swirls I took to be snakes and other carvings that may have been lizards. Then there were some squiggly lines and shapes I couldn't decipher.

"I guess we're not the first people to discover this cave," I said.

Jessie put his hand to his chest and, with complete seriousness and absolute reverence, held his other hand out and declared, "Behold, Rossi, the work of your people."

It seemed like an important moment for us, so I tried to keep a straight face, but when I saw Matthew's face, we both burst out laughing.

"Really nice, guys," Jessie grumbled. "Why you got to make fun at a time like this, I simply don't understand." He stormed off into the dark. I wondered where he thought he was going. About two seconds later we heard a loud grunt as Jessie obviously tripped over something and fell.

Matthew and I went to help him, but Rossi stayed where she was. I turned around. She still held the lantern up to the wall. She put her helmet down and reached out a hand like she was going to touch it. "Rossi?" I said.

She pulled her hand back. "Come here, Gus," she said softly.

I walked to her. "One of these things," she said, "does *not* belong."

"What?"

She stared at me. "Look." She touched my chin and turned my face toward the rock.

I scanned over the images again: deer and people and swirls and arrows and . . .

incongruous: out of place

Arrow.

I pointed at the arrow that was different. It was larger than the rest of the arrows, and, whereas the others looked like they had been carved with great care, this one seemed to have been hastily scraped onto the wall. "This."

"Right. Why do you think it's different?"

I smiled at her. "You keep asking me questions I don't know the answer to."

She shrugged her shoulders like she didn't know the answer either, and we rejoined Jessie and Matthew, who couldn't get far without the light.

I felt like I was in a science fiction movie as I gazed around the cave. It was hard to believe it was real, that someone hadn't built it. The whole place looked like it was melting all around us with large mounds of bubbling rock and long, oozing, skinny strands coming down from the ceiling so low we had to duck under some of them. The ground boiled up under our feet. Every step was an effort as we climbed over large piles of rock and clusters of stalagmites.

"Those things up there look like giant carrots." Jessie's voice sounded strange as it echoed around me. I looked up at the ceiling.

"Maybe we're under some giant's garden," Matthew said, cracking himself up.

"And those look like bacon," Jessie went on, ignoring Matthew. "And those rocks look like giant toasted marshmallows, melting over a fire. And that whole wall looks like it's covered in popcorn."

"You hungry or something?" I asked him.

"I'm always hungry." Then Jessie shrieked and swatted at the air as he ran into one of the long, skinny straws. It snapped and broke.

"Stop wrecking the cave, Jessie," I said.

As we moved on, I looked all around us at the giant columns, trying to remember things I saw in case we got lost. I pictured us walking in circles around the cave until our lights burned out. I formed a map in my mind—I imagined one column as a sumo wrestler, another as a snowman, another as a stack of tires.

Rossi walked ahead of us with the lantern. "Hey, Rossi." Matthew stepped up beside her, nearly going down as he stumbled over a loose rock. I narrowed my eyes at him, but they didn't notice.

"Hey, Rossi," Matthew said again as he regained his balance. "How do you ride like that?"

"Oh, now you want riding tips," I said.

Matthew turned and shot me an evil look. "Be quiet, Gus." He turned back to Rossi.

"Like what?" she said.

"Like, you know, how you ride. Like almost as good as Bo."

"*Almost* as good?" Rossi said. "Oh yeah, you're usu-ally too far behind to see us." Matthew let out an exas-perated sound, but Rossi smiled at him. "I don't know,

Matthew. I just ride. I don't really think about it. Riding is like breathing. If you think too much, you crash."

"No one would ever accuse Matthew of thinking too much," Jessie said, walking beside me. We ducked under a few particularly long stalactites.

Matthew ignored him. "Well, how'd you learn?"

"My dad taught me."

"Oh. Do you think he would be willing to teach me?"

"No."

Jessie and I grinned at each other as Matthew dropped his head. "Don't even take time to think about it or anything," he mumbled.

"He doesn't have time for stuff like that," she said.

Matthew walked quietly, his head still hung.

"The silt," Rossi finally said.

"Huh?" Matthew raised his head back up. "What about it?"

"You always eat it in the silt," Jessie said, grunting as we climbed over a boulder. "My favorite part of every race."

"You slow down when you hit it," she said. "If you hit it, you need to ride through as fast as possible."

"Why?"

"It's like water. If you wanted to glide over water, you wouldn't slow down. You'd sink."

"Huh." Matthew seemed to think this over. "But you never ride in the silt."

"Not if I don't have to."

"I've never seen Rossi eat it in the silt," Jessie said. "Maybe she knows what she's talking about."

"But how can you be sure there aren't any ruts or rocks under the powder?" Matthew asked.

"You can't be."

"Oh."

"And the whoops," Rossi said.

"Yeah?"

"Again, go fast so you glide over the tops as much as possible. Going slow slows you down."

"I guess I'm just being careful," Matthew said.

"Being careful doesn't win races."

"Isn't that a little scary?"

"What's there to be scared of?"

Matthew shrugged. "Having a bad crash."

"I don't crash," she said. "And there's no time for scared. Save scared for afterward."

Matthew was quiet for a moment. "Anything else? Like any other tips?"

I rolled my eyes as their conversation continued. "Rossi shouldn't be giving that jerk tips," Jessie whispered to me. "I like watching him lose."

I nodded. "I don't know why she's being so nice to him. He's never been nice to her. He was there laughing when Bo took her bike."

"Yeah, she's too nice," Jessie complained. "She should be giving him fake tips to make him crash." We quietly snickered together. "Maybe that's what she's doing," he said. "Don't think, don't be careful, go as fast as possible. Sounds like terrible advice."

I shook my head. "It's not. That's exactly how she rides."

"Whoa." Jessie threw an arm out across my chest—there was a large rock right in front of my feet. I had gotten complacent and hadn't been watching my steps well enough.

"Thanks, brother," I said before I realized it. I hadn't called Jessie brother since he started sitting at Ramiro's table. I felt embarrassed about it, too, like I didn't have the right to call him that anymore.

"You're welcome, brother." Jessie patted me on the back, and we stepped over the rock, careful not to get too far behind Rossi and lose the light. "So how come you ditched me last year?"

He had made it sound like a casual question, but I could tell from his expression he didn't feel casual about it at all. "Are you serious? You totally ditched me."

Jessie shook his head. "Nuh-uh. One day you just decided to sit with Louis instead of us. And then every day after that."

I huffed. "Yeah, well, would you want to sit at a table where you can't understand a word anyone is saying and they're always making fun of you?"

Jessie frowned. "Who was making fun of you?"

"All of you," I snapped. I was mortified to realize I was on the verge of tears. I tried to regain my composure. "Always pointing at me and laughing and saying my name." My lower lip quivered. Just a little. I bit it.

"Dude! That's because I was always telling them funny stories about stuff you've pulled. Like when you smeared peanut butter on Bo's bike seat and he looked like he pooped his pants all day. They hate that guy. They thought it was hilarious. And when you put one of your grandma's diapers on Matthew's handlebars and everyone called him Diaper Dude for like a year after that." Jessie cracked up in his funny, heaving way. It made me smile. Then I shushed him and glanced nervously at Matthew ahead of us, but he was focused on the riding tips Rossi was giving him.

"Anyway," Jessie said, "no one has ever made fun of you. Those guys think you're funny. They even asked me once why you weren't sitting with us anymore."

"Well, maybe because I can't understand anything you guys say. You totally abandoned me for them."

Jessie winced like I had physically hurt him. "I didn't abandon you, Gus. I'm not like *him*."

"I know you're not like *him*," I said. "I just thought things were good the way they were."

"Good?" Jessie said, his mouth agape. "I didn't think it was so good watching you get tortured every day. You know, strength in numbers, Gus. It can't always be just the two of us. Plus, I like those guys. They're nice and they don't let Bo bully them or me. Or you, when you were still hanging out with us."

I swallowed, blinking back my tears. "I'm glad you've made new friends," I managed to say without my voice cracking.

"I still have room for old friends. It doesn't have to be one or the other."

I sniffled and rubbed my nose. "No. No, it doesn't."

Jessie threw his head back and groaned. "Isn't this just the worst day of your life?"

Matthew stopped and turned around. "Are you serious?"

Jessie faced him. "Yeah. I am."

Matthew shook his head. "Well, lucky you."

"Oh, you've had worse days than this?" Jessie said.

"Worse than getting buried in a collapsed mine? Worse than getting trapped in a cave with no hope for escape? Worse than getting viciously attacked by millions of rabid vampire bats?"

hyperbole: extravagant exaggeration

"Just about a thousand times worse," Matthew said. "Not like you care, though."

"You're right." Jessie crossed his arms. "I don't."

Matthew shook his head and turned around. After a few steps, he was gone.

Disappeared.

Like magic.

THE THREE OF US RAN TO WHERE MATTHEW

had vanished.

crevice: a narrow opening made by splitting,
  particularly in rock or earth

I would have fallen into the large crack in the
ground myself if Jessie hadn't pulled me back.

Rossi held the lantern over the opening. Matthew
was wedged between two rock walls just a few feet
below us. All I could see below him was blackness. "Are
you okay, Matthew?" Rossi asked.

Matthew looked up at us through the narrow crevice, his face strained. "I can't move." I turned the flashlight on and shined it into the blackness—there was

another ground, covered in jagged rocks, below him. *Far* below him. Rossi and I looked at each other. She barely shook her head. I flipped off the flashlight and didn't tell Matthew what we'd seen.

"Can you try to pull yourself up?" Rossi asked.

"With what? There's nothing to grip."

"Can you reach your arms up?" she said.

Matthew slowly raised his arms over his head. "It's just my stomach that's stuck."

Rossi looked at Jessie. "Maybe you can lie down and reach him."

Jessie lay on the ground and reached into the crevice. He and Matthew gripped hands. Jessie grunted and huffed as he tried to pull him up. Matthew's face contorted in pain. "I can't move him," Jessie said.

Rossi looked at me. "Gus, you lie down and grab his other hand."

I lay down on the ground and . . . *really?*

mortification: great embarrassment or shame

"Gus can't reach me." Matthew strained to grab my hands, which were about an inch from his. "His arms are too short."

Rossi set the lantern down and lay on her stomach.

She reached Matthew's other hand. She and Jessie pulled and pulled, but Matthew wouldn't budge. They finally let go and sat at the edge of the crevice. "What do you have in your backpack?" Rossi asked me.

I shrugged. "Just my jar of water, Twinkies, and a couple of bologna sandwiches."

Rossi looked down at Matthew. "Take out the bologna sandwiches."

"What are you going to do with them?" I asked her.

She raised her eyebrows. "We're going to *eat* them. We all need strength."

I took them out and gave everyone a half. "I don't think I can eat that," Matthew said. "I can barely breathe, much less eat." I saved his half to give him later. I hoped there was a later.

When we were done eating, Rossi pulled her knees up to her chest and folded her hands in front of her face. I took out my pocket watch and checked the time—already after two. I slammed it shut. "Maybe we should shut the lantern off if we're just going to sit here," I said. "Save the batteries."

Rossi turned the lantern off, and then we were in complete darkness like I had never known. None of us spoke. That buzzing started in my ears until our breathing got heavy enough to drown it out. Rossi flipped the lantern back on.

"That was a fun experiment," said Jessie.

"You guys should just move on," said Matthew.

"No," Rossi said. "We're not leaving you here in the dark like this. Just . . . give me a moment." She pulled her hair out of its frazzled ponytail, slipped the rubber band around her wrist, and pushed her long dark hair back from her face.

Jessie let out a big dramatic sigh. As much as he disliked Matthew, I knew he agreed with Rossi. "This winning for worst day yet?" he said.

Matthew shook his head. "Nope."

Jessie scoffed. "What could be so much worse than getting stuck in a big crack in the ground in a cave with no hope of getting out? Not to mention not finding any gold. No race for either you or Rossi. Bo is totally going to win. No one here is getting a new dirt bike, and no one is going to Breaker Bradley's. All of this was for nothing!" Jessie's voice had raised to a near screech, and the word nothing echoed off the cave walls all around us.

Matthew took a labored breath. The rock must have been pushing into his diaphragm. "Valentine's Day. Second grade."

"Really?" I said. "I remember you got made fun of for giving out those cards, but really?"

"I stole those cards," Matthew said. "I stole them from the Nowhere Market and Ostrich Farm. We couldn't afford them, and I wanted to have cards to give out, since I'd never gotten to before. Not like it mattered anyway. I just got made fun of."

"There are worse things than getting made fun of for giving out stupid Valentine's cards," Jessie said.

I could only see the top of Matthew's dirty hair as he said, "My mom found out I had stolen the cards, and when I got home that day . . . When I got home, she beat me so badly with a belt I could barely walk for two days. She screamed at me that it was bad enough she was burdened with me when my dad skipped out on her. It was the worst she had ever beaten me."

I stared down at him. "The worst?"

Matthew shrugged. "I'm used to it now."

We were all quiet as Matthew took a deep breath and wiped at his cheeks.

Finally, I said, "Why do you hang out with Bo?"

Matthew took another loud breath like the air simply wouldn't fill his lungs. "I couldn't take it at home *and* at school." He wiped at his cheek again. "I just couldn't." I looked at Jessie, but he turned away from me. "There are worse things than being stuck in this cave. And there are definitely worse things than not going to Breaker Bradley's. That sort of thing is just a pipe dream for people like us anyway."

"No, it's not," I said. "Rossi could've gone. She would have won if it hadn't been for me." I looked at her, but she didn't even seem to hear me.

"You mean if it hadn't been for Bo," Jessie said. "Stop blaming yourself for what that jerk did."

"You know, Bo's not that bad," Matthew said. "Maybe he wouldn't be like he is if his dad hadn't been so terrible. That was the nastiest man I've ever known in my life."

"We all make our own choices," I said.

"Yeah," Jessie said. "None of us have had rainbows and unicorns for our lives."

Jessie's life was the closest to rainbows and unicorns of anyone I knew. But I guess that was saying a lot, too. There was no money left for any extras in Jessie's life, including a new dirt bike. And yet, I was somehow jealous of what he had.

"Anyway, I'm just saying," Matthew said, "Bo's had it bad. Real bad. The worst I've ever seen. I mean, his dad's in prison for killing his mom. Don't forget that. And Jack's pretty good with his fists, too."

I didn't want to feel sorry for Bo, and it made me annoyed with Matthew for making it happen.

"It's your turn now," Matthew said to me.

"My turn what?"

"Your worst day. I need something to distract me," Matthew took a deep breath, "from the pain."

I looked at Rossi, but she seemed lost in her own head. I thumbed through my mind's catalogue of bad days: today (or yesterday, I guess) when Bo stuck my face in a cactus, last week when Bo threw a scorpion on my head, last year when Grandma called me in sick at school and told them I had "the trots." And about a thousand more days just like those.

Or should I tell them the real worst day? I'd tried for years to never think about it. To never think about *him*. I had nearly succeeded in completely blocking those memories out. But now it was all I could think about.

"My mom took off when I was a toddler," I said. "I don't remember the day she left."

"Doesn't count," Matthew said.

"I know. It was just me and my dad until I was six. We lived in Reno. It was tough, you know, trying to work and take care of a kid on your own. He wasn't a bad dad or anything. I think he did the best he could. He didn't make a lot of money as a glazier."

"What's that?" Matthew asked.

"They work with glass—like glass windows and doors. Anyway, we ate a lot of canned food and I slept on the couch in the living room. He usually wasn't there when I got home from school, so I would watch TV until dinnertime. He'd get home and open a can of chili or something and we'd watch more TV together until he told me to go to sleep. That was pretty much my life. I thought it was a good life actually."

"Doesn't sound too bad," Matthew said from below us. "You could watch as much TV as you wanted."

"One morning he woke me up early when it was still dark and told me he had a surprise. We drove for several hours. I couldn't believe it when I saw the sign for Disneyland. I thought I was dreaming."

Rossi was still sitting in that same exact position, legs crossed, hands clasped in front of her face. She stared at nothing.

"What was it like?" Matthew asked, as he had when we first entered the cave.

"It was everything you think. I can barely even describe it."

"Try," Matthew said.

"Well, when we first walked in there was a big train station and a street that was like . . . the opposite of

Nowhere." I didn't need to explain further—they understood. "And there are different lands with all different rides." I tried to remember the names. "Space Mountain, Splash Mountain, Thunder Mountain."

"What kind of food do they have?" Matthew asked.

"My dad bought us the best corn dogs ever. And cotton candy, too. I always remember the cotton candy cost so much money, but he said it was my special day. I guess I was too young to think about the cost of the day too much, but I know it was a lot."

"Did you go on Pirates of the Caribbean?" Matthew asked.

My stomach lurched. "Yeah. Yeah, I went on it. Really, the coolest thing I'd ever seen."

Matthew grunted, and we all looked down at him as he tried to move. "I really want to go," he said.

"When we got off Pirates of the Caribbean, we stopped in this gift shop. My dad said I could pick anything I wanted. Anything at all. I knew I must be dreaming. I spent probably a whole hour searching the store, trying to pick the perfect thing. And then I found this giant barrel of sparkling treasure—jewels. You could fill a bag of them for like five dollars. I thought they were real and I would take them and sell them when we left, and then my dad and I could live in a nice place and eat nice food and he would be so much happier.

"So that's what I got. After my dad paid for them, he knelt down and told me, 'Every time you look at those jewels, you'll think of me and this day. You've had a great day, haven't you?'

"I told him it was the best day of my life. We watched the fireworks before we left, but I kept pulling out my jewels. They looked so sparkly and real by the light of the fireworks. I counted them over and over again. Seventeen. I had seventeen jewels.

"Then we left. I fell asleep in the car and didn't wake up again till it was almost morning. And we were here. In Nowhere. He pulled a couple of bags I didn't know were there out of the trunk of the car and walked me up to my grandma's trailer and knocked on the door. She knew we were coming."

forsake: to quit or leave entirely; abandon

"And that was the last time I saw my dad. The last time I ever spoke to my dad. He left me here with a woman I had never met before in my life."

Everyone was quiet. "I still have the jewels. I keep them in the table beside my bed. I take them out sometimes, trying to remember what it felt like that day—the hope I had felt when I picked them. I had thought they were real, but they were as fake as my dad. And now all I feel when I see them is . . . worthless. He bought me those jewels because he felt guilty about not wanting me, not because he loved me. Those jewels don't remind me of some great memory with him. They remind me that no one in this world wants me."

Everyone was quiet until Matthew finally said. "Geez, Gus. Couldn't you come up with something better than that?"

I smiled a little. "Sorry. Bo did give me a wedgie in front of everyone in the cafeteria once. That was really embarrassing."

"Yeah," Matthew said quietly. "Yeah, I remember that." Matthew took several rasping breaths. I looked at Rossi, but she seemed lost in thought still. What were we going to do about Matthew? "Well, we already know Jessie's worst day. What about you, Rossi?"

She finally put her hands down and looked at us. "We need lubricant."

Jessie gawked at her. "Now's a strange time to be thinking about your motorcycle."

Rossi tied the rubber band back around her hair. "Yes, I wish we had motorcycle oil. We need something to lubricate Matthew so he'll slide out more easily. Maybe your water, Gus."

I frowned. "I was kind of hoping to use that water to prevent, uh, you know, death by dehydration."

Jessie jumped up excitedly and bounced from foot to foot. "Oh, I know! Let's pee on him!"

Matthew's head shot back. "No way!"

"Would you rather stay stuck down there?" I said. Matthew looked terrified, and I wasn't sure which thought scared him more.

Rossi shook her head. "That's not slippery enough." She grabbed my backpack and started pulling the Twinkies out one by one. "These will have to do instead."

"Twinkies?" I said.

She tore open one of the small packages. She broke the cake in half and scooped out the filling with her finger. "We're going to need all of them."

The three of us scooped the filling out of each cake. Jessie and Rossi reached down and gave it to Matthew, and he did his best to shove it between his body and the rock walls while I carefully placed the leftover cakes back in the packages. No need to waste them.

"There's not a whole lot," Matthew said. "But I guess it's worth a try." He wiped the excess off as well as he could on the front of his shirt.

Jessie and Rossi lay back down on their stomachs and gripped Matthew's hands. They all three strained and grunted and pulled, but Matthew wouldn't move. Rossi stared at him, breathing heavily. "Listen to me, Matthew. You need to completely relax and let all your air out. Just go limp and let Jessie and me pull you up."

Matthew nodded at her and closed his eyes. Once his breathing evened out, he let out a long breath. Rossi looked at Jessie and they pulled. "He moved!" Jessie cried.

Matthew's eyes shot open. "Just stay calm," Rossi ordered him. He shut his eyes again.

Rossi and Jessie pulled, and Matthew slid up. When he was high enough, he grabbed the edge of the crevice and pulled himself onto the ground.

"Are you okay?" I said.

"I don't know." He stood up and stretched his arms over his head. "I kind of slid down in there, so nothing hit me too hard. I think I'm okay." He swooned a little to one side. "A little dizzy, though."

I handed Matthew his half of the bologna sandwich. "Here, eat this. It might help." He scarfed it down in a couple of bites. I pulled out my pocket watch and flipped it open. "We should probably get moving.

It's nearly three o'clock already." I snapped the pocket watch shut.

"What's that you keep looking at, Gus?" Rossi asked.

"Just my pocket watch."

"Can I see it?"

"Sure." I handed it to her, and she studied it for a moment. "W.A.D.," she whispered.

"No, it's W.D.A.," I told her.

She looked up at me. "No, Gus." Then she looked at Matthew. "What did you say your great-grandfather's name was?"

Matthew stretched a little from side to side. "William Dufort."

"Do you know what his full name was, including his middle name?" she asked.

Matthew stopped stretching and stared down at her. "William André Dufort."

She looked down at the watch. "W.A.D.," she said again. "William André Dufort."

"No, no," I said. "It's W.D.A."

"No, Gus," she said again. "The larger letter in the center stands for the last name. It's W.A.D."

"Let me see that pocket watch," Matthew said and snatched it out of Rossi's hand.

Then he looked at me, his face furious. "You little thief!" he said.

"What?"

"This is my great-grandfather's pocket watch!"

"No way."

"Yes way," Matthew said. "My dad had a belt buckle that had this same thing on it. And, trust me, I knew my dad's belt really well. Where did you get this?" He looked at Jessie. "Did you give it to him?"

"No!" Jessie cried. "Gus has always had that."

I reached for the pocket watch, but Matthew moved it away and held it over my head. "My dad gave it to me," I said as I jumped, trying to reach the watch. "And my grandma gave it to him. It belonged to her father."

"Where did *he* get it from?" Matthew demanded.

I didn't answer him as I kept jumping, trying to reach the watch. I stumbled on a rock as I came down and twisted my ankle. I winced in pain, causing Matthew to lower his arm. I jumped again and grabbed it. I couldn't pull it down, so I lifted my feet off the ground, using the full weight of my body to get his arm down. It stayed up.

Then Rossi walked up behind Matthew and snatched the pocket watch out of his hand. He dropped me and turned around. "Hey!"

Rossi ignored him as she studied the watch, running her finger around the outside like she was testing it.

"Be careful, Rossi," I told her. "The back is loose."

Rossi continued examining the watch intently. "What if the story is all wrong?" she said.

Matthew and Jessie looked at each other. "What do you mean?" Jessie asked.

"What if . . ." Rossi said. "What if there was a third person who stole the gold?" Then Rossi looked at me. "Gus, did you know your pocket watch—"

"*My* pocket watch," Matthew said.

She looked at Matthew a moment then back at me. "Did you know William Dufort's pocket watch had a secret compartment?" Rossi ran her finger around the edge of the watch and jiggled the loose backing a little. Something clicked and she popped the back open.

"Whoa," I said, stepping forward. We all gathered around the watch as Rossi lifted out a small, folded piece of paper.

"Whoa," I said again.

She carefully began to unfold the paper, but then we heard a strange rumbling sound. Rossi paused and listened.

"What was that?" Jessie's voice trembled. "Please tell me one of you just farted."

"No." I didn't think the one from twenty minutes ago counted.

Rossi continued unfolding the paper, but then we heard it again—a low rumbling that grew louder and then quieted slightly. Then it grew louder again.

Jessie raised shaking fists up to his face, his eyes clenched shut. "Oh my gosh. What *is* that? It sounds like someone's trying to start up a dirt bike in here."

Rossi stopped unfolding the paper again, and I noticed her hands shook slightly. Suddenly the soft sound grew into a full growl. I took the flashlight out of my pocket and switched it on with trembling hands.

Matthew whispered, "What is it?"

I slowly lifted the flashlight to shine it behind us, not completely sure where the sound had come from. With the way sounds echoed off the walls in this cave, it was difficult to tell where any of them came from.

I turned in a slow circle until the eyes of a large cat flashed far off in the distance.

3:00 AM

JESSIE WHIMPERED BESIDE ME. "WORST.
Day. Ever," he moaned.

Rossi slowly folded the paper back up with shaking hands, making a loud crinkling sound. She carefully pushed it and the watch into her pocket.

"Shhhhhhhh," I said to her through clenched teeth. My jaw twitched. "Quiet."

"No!" Rossi shouted at me. "Don't be quiet!" Then she started screaming and waving her arms all around. I thought for a moment she'd lost her mind, and then I remembered from a lesson at school—make noise, make yourself look big.

I grabbed her hand so it appeared we were connected and started shouting with her. I waved the flashlight around. I saw that Jessie and Matthew were moving back slowly.

"Climb those rocks right there," Rossi said to Jessie, angling her head at a massive pile of boulders next to us. "Go as high as you can."

Jessie attempted to climb the first large boulder as the cat started making its way toward us, gliding gracefully over the rocky surface. I dropped the flashlight and the three of us pushed Jessie up. He screamed and stepped on Matthew's face in his panic to get on top of the rock. Jessie reached down for Matthew. Rossi and I pushed as Jessie pulled and Matthew made it up.

I looked at Rossi. I knew she would try to argue, to make me go first. "There's no time!" I yelled at her and put my hands out linked together. She stepped quickly into them and jumped. Jessie caught one of her hands and Matthew the other.

The mountain lion made it to us just as they were pulling her up. It jumped at her legs. I swung my backpack at it, screaming as loud as I could. The lion seemed startled for a moment and backed off. I turned and jumped, the backpack slung around my arm.

I clutched Rossi's hands. Matthew and Jessie were holding her by the waist so she could lower down and reach me. They pulled her back, and I came up with her. The mountain lion jumped and bit my shoe, then fell back down again, taking my good Family Dollar generic sneaker with her.

We climbed another boulder, and then another, trying to get as high as we could. As far away from the mountain lion as we could.

When we couldn't get any higher, a low slanted rock ceiling right above our heads, I crouched on top of the boulder we were all huddled on and watched the mountain lion, visible from the lantern and flashlight still shining on the cave floor. She paced for a moment before jumping up on the first boulder with far more grace than we had. Then she jumped onto the next.

Jessie shook next me. "It's coming," he moaned.

When she made the final jump at us, I once more swung my backpack at her, connecting with her nose. She fell back down, clawing at the sides of the boulders and eventually landed on the rocky ground. She swiped at her face and shook her head, clearly not liking that.

"Yeah, you don't want to mess with us!" Jessie screamed. He sounded like he was hyperventilating. I worried he might fall off the rock if he passed out. With the way my heart was beating, I worried *I* might fall off the rock.

I grabbed him. "Let's sit down. Be quiet. Maybe she'll lose interest and leave."

The lion sniffed Rossi's helmet, which was still sitting near the crack Matthew had fallen into. "Please don't eat it," Rossi begged the cat.

We all sat down close together in a tight circle. "That was pretty awesome, Gus," said Matthew.

"It was daring," said Rossi.

"Yeah, Gus," said Jessie. "I think you might really be part Viking."

"You think?" I said. "*Arrrrrr.*"

"That's a pirate," said Jessie. "Not a Viking."

Oh yeah. *Duh.*

"What does a Viking say anyway?" said Matthew.

The four of us sat quietly, thinking. Finally Rossi said, "Hi, I'm a Viking."

The four of us giggled as quietly as possible, our hands over our mouths, listening to the sounds of the large cat at the base of the boulders.

We huddled closely together on the rock. We could barely see one another in the dim light from below. The mountain lion seemed to tire of pacing after a while and lay down, licking her paws and sighing loudly. "I guess we'll have to wait until she goes away," I said.

"Man," Jessie complained. "You guys should have turned off the lights. Now the batteries will get wasted.

"Gee," I said. "Sorry I didn't think of that while the lion was biting my foot off."

"Just your shoe," Jessie mumbled. He was cranky. He always got that way when he hadn't had enough to eat.

Despite the half of a bologna sandwich I'd eaten, I was still really hungry, too. I opened my backpack and pulled out the empty Twinkies.

"Don't!" Matthew whispered. "It will smell the food. That's probably what attracted it in the first place."

"I don't think mountain lions are into Twinkies," I said. "It was probably the bologna."

"I bet it'd like to eat Matthew's Twinkie," Jessie said, totally cracking himself up.

"I bet it'd like to eat you, Jesus," Matthew said. "I mean your whole body. Because your whole body is like a Twinkie."

We all stared at Matthew. "That took way too long to explain," I said.

I took a swig of my warm pickle water, which had miraculously survived the cave-in, bats, and mountain lion. I passed it around so the others could have a drink.

Then I handed out the empty, smashed Twinkies, and the cave filled with the sounds of crinkling as we all reopened the packages and hungrily scarfed the leftovers down.

"These sure would have been a lot better with some filling in them." Jessie glowered at Matthew. "If only someone hadn't stupidly fallen into a big crack."

"You better hope I don't stupidly put a big crack in your head." Matthew shook his fist at Jessie.

I let out a sigh. "Please don't get in a fight up on this rock." They quieted down.

When we had finished our Twinkies, Rossi pulled the paper out of her pocket and opened it. "What do you think it is?" Jessie asked.

Rossi shook her head. "I have no idea." She held the paper in front of her face from different angles. "I can't tell. I can barely see."

"How did your dad get that pocket watch, Gus?" Matthew said.

"My grandma gave it to him."

"And how did she get it?"

"I told you—it was her dad's."

"How did *he* get it?" Matthew asked.

"I don't know. She said it had been her daddy's. She said he was a drunken idiot who got bitten by a rattlesnake and died in the desert when she was just a little girl on the night . . ."

"On what night?" Matthew asked.

happenstance: coincidence

Probably not.

I swallowed. "On the night that William Dufort went into the mine and died."

Matthew and Jessie gave each other excited looks. "But that watch was the only thing he had on him when he died," I told them. "And the only darn thing he left my grandma, or so she said. She said he probably found it while he was drinking out in the desert."

"Maybe he stole it," Matthew said. "Maybe he stole it and everything else."

"Or maybe he found it, just like my grandma said," I answered.

"Maybe that paper is a treasure map," Jessie said excitedly.

"Yeah, and maybe it's a grocery shopping list," Matthew said.

Jessie frowned. "Why would someone put a grocery shopping list in a pocket watch?"

I looked at Rossi. "What do you think it is?"

She shrugged. "Could be anything." Then she turned her head. "Do you feel that?"

"Feel what?" I asked.

She stood up, hunched over, and held out a hand. "I feel air movement."

"So?" Matthew said.

"So that means there could be an opening nearby." Rossi jumped down to a lower boulder, and then to one next to it near a wall of the cave. She pulled herself up onto a ledge. I could barely see her as she walked along the ledge and disappeared into the darkness.

"Rossi," I called out.

"I see light," she said. "Come here."

I looked down at the lights on the ground. I didn't want to get too far away from them. The mountain lion was still down there, looking bored.

I jumped from one boulder to the next as Rossi had, then climbed up onto the ledge with her. There was a small hole in the wall, and when I stuck my head in it, I could see a dim light. "You're right. We can get out!" I called to the boys. They followed us until they were standing underneath the ledge.

"Actually," Rossi squeezed into the hole and then back out, "*we* can get out. It's not big enough for them. It's barely big enough for us."

Matthew and Jessie groaned on the boulder. "Are you serious?" Jessie said. "We have to stay here?"

"We'll go get help," I told them. "Just stay on that rock and wait. We'll get help and come back for you."

Rossi was already tying her T-shirt into a knot, getting ready to enter the hole. "It's difficult to tell, but I think it's maybe only fifteen feet to get out. We can make it."

My stomach cramped. The idea of squeezing through that hole and somehow inching my way fifteen feet was about as appealing as Grandma telling everyone in town, in the entire state of Arizona, that I was home with "the trots."

"Are you prepared to do this, Gus?"

Pfft. Like I would tell her no and have her think I was a total wimp. I took a deep breath. "Follow me, Rossi. I'll go first in case there's anything in there."

I couldn't see her face in the dim light as she whispered, "Okay."

Before I squeezed into the hole, Matthew called, "Be careful, Gus."

"Yeah, man," Jessie added. "Be careful. There could be, like, a rattlesnake den in there or something."

I grimaced. "Gee, thanks."

"Don't worry," Jessie assured me, "they won't bite

you if you don't bother them." I looked at the tiny hole—if anything was in there, I would definitely be bothering it.

I squeezed myself into the small opening and started shimmying forward on my belly like a snake, my arms out in front of me. I willed myself not to panic and turned my mind to other things—the horrible movie I watched on TV a couple of nights ago about killer tomatoes, Matthew stealing Valentine's cards, Jessie and I sitting on his trailer's front porch drinking his mom's homemade horchata, which I hadn't had in nearly a whole year. I suddenly wanted a glass of horchata really bad.

But mostly I thought of Rossi, also inching her way through the rocky hole behind me. Rossi standing in the desert, her hair plastered to her cheek, trading Loretta for me. Rossi racing. If she never got to race again, it would be my fault.

My pants caught on a sharp rock and tore right in the crotch as I moved forward. "Great," I muttered. There went four dollars down the toilet. I mean, they were already ripped up from climbing the rubble, but now they were unwearable.

"You okay?" I heard Rossi say behind me.

"Yeah, I tore my pants. Again. For like the millionth time."

Rossi breathed heavily. "My shirt's torn. And my pants. And I think I tore some of my hair out, too."

"Don't worry. We're almost there. I see the opening up ahead."

The opening actually looked really far away still. And the hole felt really small.

"Tell me something." Rossi's voice was getting more breathless with every word.

"About what?"

"Anything," she said. "Anything."

Of course my mind went totally blank. "Uh," I stuttered. "How am I going to buy your bike back without any gold?"

"I don't care about my bike right now. All I care about . . . is getting out . . . of this hole." She breathed so heavily, I worried she would pass out.

"Are you okay, Rossi?"

"Just talk about something else."

"I hope we can make it back without water." I cringed. That was a terrible thing to make her worry about right now.

"We just drank and it's still dark out. We'll be fine."

I tried to think of something else to say. "I hope my grandma doesn't wake up and call the police when she finds me gone."

"Don't worry about that."

"They'll think we all died in the mine collapse," I said.

Rossi was quiet for a moment. "Do you really think so?"

"Well, Bo would hopefully eventually tell them that's where we went and then they'd see the mine had collapsed in a new area. They'd probably think we were dead."

"If we get out of here," she said, "we could leave Nowhere."

I stopped. "Rossi?"

"No one would search for us. Like you said."

I moved forward again as I thought about that. I was almost to the opening. "Where would we go?"

"Baja."

"As in Mexico?"

"Yes."

"Why? Are you running from the law?" I joked.

Rossi let out a breathy laugh behind me. "Maybe."

I was finally there. I pushed myself out of the hole onto another narrow ledge. I turned around and reached my hand out for Rossi. Her dark hair was gray with dust and rocks, a shiny film of sweat on her face. She grabbed my hand and squeezed out of the hole onto the ledge with me. We breathed heavily as we stood and looked at each other. We had finally made it out.

THE SKY WAS SO BRIGHT FROM THE FULL

moon, I worried the sun might be coming up already. Rossi removed my watch from her pocket and handed it to me. From the light of the moon, I could see it was after four o'clock.

I looked down. The cliff below us was completely vertical, and the desert floor may as well have been twenty miles below, instead of the twenty or so feet it actually was.

I felt something touch my hand. Rossi entwined her fingers with mine for a moment before letting go. She sat down on the ledge and swung her legs over the side.

I sat next to her and nervously let my legs hang down as well, hoping we didn't slip off. I shook my head. We didn't need to talk about it. We both knew there was no getting down from here. If we tried to jump it, we'd probably break our legs or ankles. Then we'd just lie there until we died of dehydration. Or got eaten by something. The desert was an unforgiving place.

Rossi pulled the paper out of her pocket and once more attempted to read it. "It's too faded," she said. "I can't make anything out. I need better light." She folded it and put it back in her pocket.

I knew we didn't have unlimited time, but I also knew neither of us could handle going right back in that hole. "It's good to be outside," I said, breathing a little more easily now. This was the coolest time of day, but I bet the temperature was still ninety.

Rossi stared out at the dimly lit landscape. We could see the lights of Casa Grande way off in the distance. "I love the desert at night," she finally said. "Everything is silver when there's a full moon."

I turned to her. "What's in Baja?"

She picked a rock out of her hair. "The Baja One Thousand."

"Oh. What's that?"

"It's a long race through the Baja peninsula. A thousand-mile race. Anyone can enter—anyone in the world. And you can use any kind of vehicle—buggy, truck, motorcycle. Most people ride in some kind of truck, but you could do it in your grandma's station wagon if you wanted to."

I smiled. "You want to do it on a dirt bike, don't you?"

"Of course."

"But why? I mean, why the Baja One Thousand instead of a bigger Supercross competition?"

She shrugged. "Like I said, anyone can enter. It doesn't matter who you are, how much money you have, or what you drive. It doesn't matter that you're a girl. You don't win much money. People don't do it for money; they do it for love—love of racing, love of the desert, love of competition. There are no pretentions. No bimbos in skimpy bikinis holding up signs." She shot me a sideways glance, like she was checking to make sure I also disapproved of bimbos in skimpy bikinis holding up signs.

I made my very best disgusted face and nodded in agreement.

"The people who finish in one hundredth place celebrate as much as the people who finish first . . . maybe even more. It's about proving you can conquer Baja. Proving you're more than what people think.

That you're not just some piece of discarded trash."
She looked at me. "Though you have been discarded.
Haven't you, Gus?"

> **discard:** to get rid of someone or something
>   as no longer useful or desirable

Her stare made me uncomfortable. "Yes," I said.
"Are you going to let someone else's actions define
who you are or what you're worth?"
I defined words all the time. I was obsessed with
defining words. But I had never thought about how I
defined myself.

> **Gus:** nugatory, derisory, forsaken, discarded
>   nincompoop

When I didn't answer Rossi's question, she said,
"I'll be defined by what I do in this life, not by what
anyone else does to me or says about me. None of that
matters. All that matters is what *I* do." She stared into
me, like she could see my darkest thoughts. "We're not
what people have done to us, Gus. We can be whatever
we want."
I wished that were true. But could two kids in

Nowhere really be whatever they wanted? I wasn't so sure.

"What are you going to be?" I asked her.

"I don't know yet. But I know what I'm going to do. I'm going to get out of Nowhere. I'm going to make it to Baja. Somehow. And I'm going to do all one thousand miles by myself. No team. Just me and my bike in one of the most desolate, quiet, scary, amazing deserts on earth. That's all I need. People always disappoint you. My bike has never let me down."

I picked up a small pebble from the ledge and rolled it between my thumb and finger. "How will you do all thousand miles on one tank of gas? And what if you get a flat tire?"

She pursed her lips. "Yes, I'll have to have a pit crew." She sighed. "I always thought my dad would be there, that he would be my crew chief. But I don't think he cares about that anymore. Not like I do anyway."

I threw the pebble. It made a small clacking sound on the rocks below. "I bet he cares about you, though. I'm sure he'll still want to be your crew chief. And I'll join your pit crew."

She smiled. "You'd like Baja. I've heard you can smell the ocean in the desert."

"I've never smelled the ocean before. I wouldn't even know what it was I was smelling."

"You'd know."

I tried to imagine smelling the ocean in the middle of the Mexican desert. I doubted that would ever happen. The closest I'd probably ever get to seeing the ocean was *National Nerdographic*. "But is it dangerous?"

"Yes, it is. Sometimes people die. But everyone has to die sometime. I hope I die on my bike."

"I hope you don't die at all."

"That's not very likely, Gus. No one can live forever."

"Aren't you afraid to die?"

"What's there to be afraid of?"

I shrugged. "I don't know. Pain. Whatever comes after. Darkness. Just not being here anymore."

"I don't feel pain." But I didn't believe her. Everyone felt pain, didn't they? Or was it possible to stop feeling it if you got hurt enough?

I'm used to it now, Matthew had said.

"And I don't care whether I'm here or not." She swung her legs and kicked at the rock wall below us. "What's so great about being here anyway?"

I didn't know how to answer that. "I just guess if this is all there is, then . . ."

Rossi looked at me expectantly. But I didn't want to finish my sentence. I remembered how I'd felt when I thought I might never see my room again. I didn't want to tell her I didn't care whether I was here or not, either. Because I didn't want that to be true. And I really didn't want this to be all there was.

She leaned in like she was going to tell me a secret, and as though she had read my mind, she whispered, "There's more than this, Gus."

I didn't know if she was talking about this life or the next. But I think I hoped for both.

"Look." Rossi pointed at something in the distance. "Javelina."

I turned my head and saw a herd of javelina traveling toward the mountain. The moonlight was bright enough that I could make out a few babies. I looked at Rossi. She watched them, her lip tilted up just a little at one corner.

"I didn't know you and Jessie were so close," I said.

She turned to me, the faint smile already gone from her face. "Why do you say that?"

I shrugged. "Just that he went and told you about what I was doing and you came here together."

Rossi was quiet. She stared at me, a strange look

on her face. After a moment, she looked away. "Gus, my dad works two jobs. Do you understand what that means?"

I shook my head slightly.

"It means he gets up while it's still dark to go to his job at the Center for Youth. Then he goes straight to the gas station near Casa Grande to work all evening. I never, ever see him."

I didn't know what to say, so I asked her, "What does he do at the Center?"

She took her hair out of its frazzled ponytail and started running her fingers through it like a comb. "He's a social worker."

"Oh. What's a social worker?"

"He works with the boys there. He counsels them." Rossi picked a rock out of her hair and tossed it into the dark desert. "My dad says when the boys come out of that place, they're not the same as when they went in. And not better. He wants to change that. The Center doesn't give them much more than four walls and a bed, but at least they have my dad."

Just starin' at four walls.

I would go crazy.

"It's just his first year, so he doesn't get paid a lot,"

Rossi went on. "He's working to save people's lives, but he still has to work at a stupid gas station all night so *we* can afford to live."

Rossi pushed her smoothed hair over her shoulders. "It's tough, you know. Leaving home. Leaving the people I've known my whole life. Moving here, to a new place. Being alone all the time. Not everyone at school has been exactly nice to me. And, honestly, I haven't had much interest in making friends with anyone, either. It's hard to make new friends when your heart is still back home with your old friends."

"Can't you go back for a visit?" I asked her.

Rossi shrugged. "Two hundred miles takes time, which my dad doesn't have much of. And it takes expensive gas."

An owl hooted nearby, and Rossi shook her head. "Anyway, I see Jessie's mom at the scrapyard all the time, so one day she invited me to eat dinner with them since my dad's always working. I eat dinner with them a lot. Jessie's mom and I . . ." Rossi paused a moment. "We have a lot in common, I think. I really like her."

My chest suddenly hurt, and not from all the rocks that had battered it. "I know. I miss that family." Then I looked at her. "Why do you see her at the scrapyard all the time?"

Rossi ignored my question. Instead, she said, "Jessie misses you, too. He talks about you all the time."

"Really?"

"Oh, yeah. His mom's always asking him, 'Where's Gus? Where is that funny guy? What happened to you two?'"

I waited. When she didn't go on, I asked, "And what does he say?"

"He says, 'He'll be back soon. He can't stay away for long.'"

I was suddenly aware of how dry my throat felt as I tried to swallow. I was terrified my eyes would start tearing up, but nothing came. I was probably too dehydrated.

He can't stay away for long. Jessie was right. I was the one who had ditched him.

I cleared my throat. "I'm sorry your dad's never around."

Rossi gave a casual shrug. "It's okay. I can take care of myself. I don't need him like they do." But I wasn't buying it. I would have given anything to see my dad again. To have him here to take care of me. Or just to talk to me.

"My dad is going to save everybody else, Gus." She took a deep breath as she tied the rubber band back around her hair. "But one day I'm going to ride away from here on my bike and all you'll see is my dust." She tossed her hair back behind her and then clenched her fists in her lap. "I'm going to save myself."

I knew exactly what she meant. No one was going to swoop into Nowhere and rescue us. There was no top-secret government agency that was going to kidnap us. No one was going to give us a chance; we had to make our own chances. I guess a dirt bike was one way out of Nowhere. The SAT was another.

"Me too," I said.

"I know you will." She gently kicked my foot with the missing shoe. "I've seen how dauntless you can be."

dauntless: showing fearlessness and determination

"Anyway," she said, "the thought that I could win a trip to that camp—that's the only thing that's gotten me through this year. There's no other way I could ever do something like that. And I had the silly thought that maybe if I could get there, do the impossible, then who knows what could happen? Maybe someone would notice me. Maybe help me find a sponsor to get to Baja one day. But nobody notices you when you're living in a hole." She shook her head. "There's no doing the impossible for us, Gus. Now I just want to go home."

I cringed at her words. And it was my fault. My fault. *Worthless, worthless, worthless.*

I was almost too ashamed to look at her. When I finally did, I found her staring at me, a pained, almost angry expression on her face. Because of what I had done, I was sure. What I had caused. "Don't," she said firmly.

I was thankful I was so dehydrated that tears couldn't come. "Don't what?" I asked, my voice unsteady.

A pack of coyotes started crying way off in the distance. "Three times." She whipped up three fingers. "Three times you've stood up for me to Bo." She put down two fingers, still holding one up. "The first time—two hundred fifty-two days ago. Bo was furious I had beaten him a second time. He was yelling in my face, calling me a cheater, when you cried out that I hadn't cheated. He stopped yelling, and you ran. He chased you down and pushed your face into the dirt." She reached out a hand to touch a fading scar on my cheek. "You had a scab here for nearly three weeks afterward."

She pulled her hand away and held up two fingers this time. "The second time—one hundred twenty days ago. Bo was kicking my bike after a race and you yelled at him to stop. He punched you in the stomach. I watched as you lay on the ground moaning in pain. I didn't say anything to you or Bo." She cleared her throat and grimaced. "I'm ashamed of that. I've thought about it every day since."

She looked away from me. "The third time," she whispered. "Eleven hours ago." She looked at me. "And here we are."

"Here we are."

"I couldn't just watch again. I couldn't *not* do something when I had the power. I swore after I saw him punch you in the stomach, I would never just stand and watch again. I'm not nearly as big or strong as Bo, but I swore I would do whatever it took to stop him from hurting you. You repeatedly risked beatings to stand up for me when no one else would. So I knew I had to risk something, too."

"I think it would have been better if I'd kept my mouth shut all those times. It didn't help anything. And we wouldn't be here now. You'd have a real shot at going to Breaker Bradley's. Everything would be different."

The coyotes' cries grew louder, like they were heading in our direction. "There are worse things than losing a dirt bike," she said. "People . . . People are more important than metal and rubber."

"But I thought you said people always disappoint you."

She tilted her head a little. "It's possible to believe both, Gus."

"Still . . ."

"Still . . ." She leaned over and bumped me with her shoulder. "It wouldn't have been better." Then she pushed herself back away from the ledge. "I'm so tired." She laid her head against the rocky side of the mountain and closed her eyes. "Can't we just rest for a minute?"

I leaned back beside her, and she let her head fall onto my shoulder. Her hair tickled my cheek and smelled like the cave—cool, clean, fresh earth, and rock. "Rossi?" My eyes felt heavier than they ever had in my life.

"Hm?" she said faintly.

"Why do you love riding so much?"

"Because..." Her voice trailed off. I nudged her a little to keep her awake. "It feels like flying." Her raspy voice was slow from sleepiness. "Like I'm flying along. And I can forget this town . . . this life . . . this everything." She breathed in slowly. "That's the best feeling

. . . in the world. Even if it only lasts . . . for a minute. Before I have to come back."

And then it was quiet except for the cries of the coyotes slowly fading. I couldn't keep my eyes open any longer, so I allowed myself to close them. But only for a minute. Before I had to come back.

repose: the state of being at rest; sleep

"GUS!" ROSSI WAS SHAKING ME. "GUS! Wake up!"

I opened my eyes. "What? What's going on?"

"We fell asleep! The sun is up!"

I felt disoriented as I shielded my eyes from the sunlight. For a moment, I couldn't remember where I was. Then I looked down and saw the desert ground far below us. I stood up carefully and took out my pocket watch. "It's after six already."

"Now we can see what this paper is," Rossi said as she quickly pulled it out and unfolded it. She shook her head as she looked down at it. Then she held it up to the sun.

"What is it?"

She studied it awhile. Finally she said. "It *is* a map."

I laughed. "Jessie will be so excited. What's it a map of?"

She looked at me. "It's a map of the cave." She pointed at a spot on the map. "This is where we were, where Matthew went into the ground. You can see there's another huge cavern below it." She pointed at another spot on the map. "I think this is where the bats were and where the mine collapsed."

I pointed at one side of the map. "What do you think this big shaded area is?"

Rossi shook her head. "I don't know, but maybe we should try to avoid it."

"Yeah," I agreed. I wasn't thrilled at the prospect of facing the unknown, especially a big, dark, shaded unknown.

Rossi pointed at another spot on the map. "This is marked as an exit, but I think that's where another big section of the mine caved in." She looked at me excitedly. "Do you think William Dufort knew about the cave and made this map?"

"Maybe."

Her mouth opened and shut. Opened and shut. "Maybe he didn't die in the mine collapse at all. Maybe he went into the mountain."

I smiled. "You have a lot of interesting theories."

I looked down at the map. "It's cool and all," I said. "But it doesn't seem to really tell us anything very important."

"See this?" Rossi said. "Over here: A.L. What do you think that means? I think it's close to where we came in."

I thought for a moment. "Angry ladies. We should probably avoid that area, too."

Rossi ignored my joke, too focused on the map. "This other area right here is circled, but it's not labeled. I wonder what's there." Shaking her head, she folded the map back up and put it in her pocket. "Too bad there wasn't another exit marked."

I gazed at the distant city of Casa Grande, which had been so bright and shining in the moonlight. It was barely visible in the glaring sunlight now, just a brown mirage in the distance. I wished there were some way for me to fly off this mountain, but I knew I had to go back in the horrible hole.

"It won't be as bad going back," I assured Rossi.

She shook her head. "No. It will be worse because this time we're going toward dark instead of light."

I shuddered at Rossi's words before crouching down and squeezing into the hole.

It didn't take long for the panic to set in as I stared

ahead at the darkness. "Now's your turn to tell me something," I said.

Rossi breathed heavily behind me. "I'm not a thief," she finally said.

I stopped to catch my breath. "What?" I asked her.

"I don't care what Matthew or anyone thinks. But I want you to know—I'm not a thief."

I continued inching forward. "I never thought for a moment you were."

Rossi wheezed in and out a few times. "It's scrap metal."

"What?" I asked again.

"I get money by selling scrap metal to the scrap-yard. You know, people treat this area of the desert like their own personal garbage can—car parts and bed frames and pipes and even old trailer parts and everything you can imagine. They just toss it out in the desert. I haul it in on my bike and sell it. I don't think people realize that metal is valuable. Copper is the most valuable, but I almost never find any of that. Aluminum and steel are worth something, though, and there's quite a bit of that out there. Plus, it cleans up the desert. Sometimes I haul in material I know isn't worth anything just because I can't stand to look at it."

Now that I thought about it, I *had* seen her pulling

stuff behind her bike and had wondered more than once what the heck she was doing dragging garbage around.

industrious: diligent and hard-working

"That's smart, Rossi. *You're* smart."

"Well, I don't know about that." She took a deep, wheezing breath behind me. "I just know about metal."

I was already at the end. I pushed myself out back into the dark of the cave. I reached for Rossi in the blackness. She grabbed my hands, and I helped her crawl back onto the ledge. Once she was out, the light from the opening lit up the cave around us. We stood and stared at each other, still grasping hands, our breath gradually evening out. "You know about a lot of things," I told her.

I let go of Rossi's hands and searched for Matthew and Jessie. All I found was my backpack lying on the rock. They were gone.

"Man," I cried. "They had one job. One job—sit here and wait." I looked below us. "Lion's gone."

"Maybe it ate them," Rossi said, and even though it wouldn't really be funny if Matthew and Jessie had been eaten alive by the mountain lion, I laughed a little. "Lantern and flashlight are gone, too. But there's your shoe."

"And your helmet." I scanned the ground below us. "They must be somewhere around here. I guess we better get down."

I slipped my backpack over my shoulders, even though there wasn't anything useful left in it. A new backpack wasn't an option in my life, and I didn't want to be one of the kids who had to bring their stuff to school in a garbage bag. We jumped from boulder to boulder until we got to the lowest one. I helped ease Rossi down then turned around and slid off the large rock. I fell back and Rossi tried to catch me, but we both tumbled to the cave floor, rocks digging into every part of me.

Rossi grunted. "I think I landed on your shoe." She reached under herself and pulled it out.

I took my shoe from her and slipped it back on. Thank goodness it got saved, even if it now had tooth marks in it. Actually, the tooth marks made the cheap shoes feel cooler somehow, like a tough scar.

I got up and brushed the dirt from my ripped clothing. I looked down at my AT LEAST IT'S A DRY HEAT T-shirt. It was so ripped and stained the words were no longer readable. So basically, the shirt had been improved.

"I don't think I'll be wearing this again," I said.

Rossi fingered her own ripped T-shirt. "No."

The area we were standing in was lit up by the daylight coming in through the hole—a little island of light. Rossi sighed. "We're stuck."

"So stupid leaving the boulder," I mumbled. "Stupid, stupid, stupid."

Then I heard distant footsteps. Quick ones. And lots of them. Then Jessie's voice. "Run!" he cried.

Then Matthew: "Pigs!"

Rossi and I stood frozen. Matthew and Jessie were running straight for us, the light of the tiny flashlight moving around spastically in Jessie's hand, followed by the largest herd of javelina I'd ever seen in my life.

Rossi grabbed my arm and pulled me in the other direction. We ran into the dark, but the javelina were soon under our feet. One even butted me in the butt, a feat only possible for the stubby pig because of my short legs. I stumbled to the ground and covered my head with my arms as they stampeded around me.

When it was finally quiet, and I had moved each of my limbs around to make sure they weren't broken, I jumped up. "Rossi," I said. I felt on the verge of panic, being in the dark, not knowing where anyone was.

"Technically, javelina are peccaries," Rossi said in the dark, breathing hard. "Not pigs."

"Thanks for the science lesson, Ms. Rossi . . . teacher . . . lady," I heard Matthew say from somewhere.

A light flipped on not far from us, and we turned to find Jessie and Matthew clinging to a wall behind us. "Are the peckers gone?" Jessie asked.

"They're gone," Rossi said. "It's safe to come down now."

Matthew and Jessie slowly got down from the wall. "Why'd you guys leave?" I said.

They looked at each other. "We fell asleep for a while," Matthew said. "Don't know how long. Then we heard this snorting. It was totally freaking us out—" Jessie elbowed him. "I mean, we were curious to find out what it was, and then we saw this cute little baby javelina below us. It started running away, so we followed it, thinking, you know, it might be a way out. But then a bunch of big javelina came out of nowhere and chased us. And that's when we ran back into you. We were only gone for like two minutes. How long were you gone? What time is it?"

"It's after six," I said. "We were gone for a couple of hours."

"Did you get out?" Jessie asked.

"Yeah," I said. "But the hole just led to a ledge on the side of the mountain. There was no way for us to get down."

Jessie's shoulders slumped. "You think someone could hear you if you yelled?"

"I think we're still at least a mile from town based on where we were on the mountain. I don't think anyone could hear us from there. But the good news is we seem to be moving closer to town instead of farther away."

"What does that matter if we never get out?" Matthew said.

"We're going to get out," I assured him. "All these animals get in and out. So will we." I looked from Matthew to Jessie. "Where's the lantern?"

Jessie shook his head. "Burned out, man. It's gone. I dropped it when the javelina came at us because it was useless anyway."

I breathed in. "You mean all we have for light is that little flashlight?"

"Until it burns out, too," said Matthew.

"We'll be stuck in here in the dark," said Jessie. "We need to get out of here."

I opened the pocket watch and checked the time.

"You're probably right. Maybe we should go in the direction the pigs came from. They probably left a trail."

"Did you guys see what was on that paper?" Matthew asked.

"Oh, yeah," I said. "It's kind of cool. It's a map of the cave."

Jessie's face lit up. I knew he would be thrilled about guessing right. "I told you it was a map!"

"Then we can get out," Matthew said.

I shook my head. "No. The only exit marked leads to a collapsed area of the mine. It's probably blocked."

"Let me see that pocket watch." Jessie snatched it out of my hand. He shined the flashlight on it while we continued debating what to do.

"I vote for the pigs," I said.

"Me, too," said Rossi.

"Okay," Matthew said. "The pig way."

We all looked at Jessie. "Hey, do you think the person who made that map scratched this stuff onto the watch?" he said.

"Scratched what stuff?" I looked at the watch in Jessie's hand. "I've never seen any stuff scratched."

"Here," Jessie said. "Inside the secret compartment. It says 'A.L.'s nose.' Whatever that means."

I looked at Rossi. "A.L.?"

Rossi opened the paper again and we shined the flashlight on it. "Here," she said. "Not far from where we first came in, which is here," she said softly to herself. "And here are the petroglyphs. There's an arrow here." She stopped and looked up at me.

"What?" I asked her.

"That arrow," she said. "The one on the rock. It was pointing in the direction of A.L. It's this one here." She looked at Jessie. "Maybe it *is* a treasure map."

Matthew eyed me. "But who made the map? Gus's great-grandfather or mine?"

"Does it really matter?" Rossi said. "Something is here, at A.L.'s nose. Something important enough to leave clues on how to get there." Rossi looked at me, her eyes huge and glowing in the flashlight.

"Gold," I said.

She nodded excitedly. "I think so, too."

Jessie shuffled from foot to foot, shaking his head. "I don't know about going back where we were, man. If this flashlight burns out we'll never get out."

"It's worth a try, isn't it?" I said.

Jessie was now hopping from foot to foot. "We don't even know what A. L. means."

"Maybe we'll know when we get there," I said.

"And maybe we'll all die in the dark!" Jessie cried.

So dramatic.

"I tell you what," I said, "if it even flickers once, we'll get out of here. The last thing I want is to be stuck here in the dark." I shivered at the thought.

"What about the race?" said Matthew.

"We can't get Rossi's bike back without any gold, so that doesn't even matter," I said.

"It does matter," Matthew said. "I can still race."

Jessie snorted. "Yeah, race and lose."

Matthew stared at the ground and mumbled, "That's not . . . totally . . . not true." He looked at Jessie. "But at least I'm not such a bad racer that I destroyed my bike."

"That wasn't my fault," Jessie whined. "I hit a rut in the silt."

Matthew gaped at Jessie. "And how is that not your fault?"

"Enough," I said. "Let's vote on it. Raise your hand if you want to go find a bag of gold, potentially enough to buy whatever we want, including new dirt bikes for everyone."

Rossi and I raised our hands.

Jessie and Matthew looked at each other. I hoped I had brainwashed them well enough with the promise of new dirt bikes.

They slowly raised their hands.

7:00 AM

"APE LOLLIPOPS," SAID JESSIE.

"Astronaut legs," said Matthew.

"Anteater lice," said Jessie.

"Apple lemons," said Matthew.

Jessie stopped and stared at Matthew. "Apple lemons? That's not even a thing."

"Oh, and ape lollipops are?" Matthew said. "How about annoying Latinos?"

Jessie glared at Matthew. "How about agitated Latinos?"

agitated: feeling or appearing troubled or
  nervous

I smiled at Jessie. "Nice, man. But it's none of those things. Obviously. And it has a nose."

"Annoying Latinos have noses," said Matthew.

"This annoying Latino is about to punch *your* nose," said Jessie. "I mean agitated Latino." Then Jessie jumped up and down, raising his hand like we were in school. "Oh, I know, I know! Andy Letterman."

We all snickered. Andy Letterman was one of the richest kids in Nowhere—he lived in a *double-wide* trailer and wore clothes from *Target*. He was a total snob about it, too, like he was so much better than everyone else because his shirts cost two for ten dollars instead of ten for two dollars.

"I bet we'll find him just standing there in one of his fancy T-shirts looking down his nose at us," Jessie said. Then he frowned. "That would be really disappointing."

Rossi studied the map and turned around in a circle. "This map is hard to read. And it's so dark in here."

I stood beside her and stared at the map. I nodded and squinted my eyes like I was working something out, when really I was working *nothing* out. It looked mostly like a bunch of squiggly lines to me.

"Why don't you just use your Indian sense, Rossi?" Matthew asked.

Rossi dropped the map and narrowed her eyes at him. "My Indian sense?"

"Yeah, you know," Matthew said. "Like how you guys are all one with nature and the spirit world and all that. You know things that regular people don't."

"Regular people?" Rossi asked.

"Yeah," said Matthew. "It's like how animals can sense things. Or babies."

"It's like how animals can sense babies?" said Rossi.

"No. It's like how animals *and* babies can sense things. Like ghosts and stuff. Indians are like that, too."

"Oh, yes." Rossi nodded her head. "My *Indian* sense. Wait a moment. I think my Indian sense is telling me something right now." She closed her eyes and pointed both fingers at her temples, the map in one hand. "Yes. Yes, thank you, wise Indian sense." She opened her eyes and looked at Matthew. "My Indian sense has just informed me that you still wet the bed."

Jessie and I both giggled, but Matthew's mouth dropped open. "It did not!"

Rossi held up a hand. "Do not argue with wise Indian sense."

"Why would you think such a stupid thing anyway?" Jessie said.

Matthew looked at the ground and kicked at a rock. "I don't know. The movies."

"You need to watch better movies," Rossi said.

Matthew sulked while Rossi continued studying the map. "I think the petroglyphs are this way," she said.

As we worked on climbing over a large slanted boulder, Matthew said, "So Rossi, you never did tell us about your worst day."

Rossi pursed her lips, concentration on her face, as she clung to the side of the boulder. "You don't have to," I told her.

We slid down the boulder then walked quietly for a few minutes before Rossi finally said, "I lived on the reservation until last year. My mom died when I was four, so my dad mostly raised me. We didn't have much, but that was okay. Back then he spent a lot more time with me. He taught me how to ride a dirt bike. Taught me how to fix a dirt bike. Taught me everything I know about them. He was a great rider and wanted me to be just like him." She laughed. "He even started a Tohono O'odham chapter of this national motorcycle club for Indians. Riders would come from all over for our pow-wows. It was so much fun."

Rossi cleared her throat. "And he always called me his little Rossi." She glanced at Matthew. "Because Rossi is the best."

Matthew smiled at her. "I think so, too."

She cleared her throat. "Anyway, he said that he and I were going to go on a great adventure on motorcycles. That we would make it all the way to Baja. Then one day a boy we knew, a friend of mine, got thrown into the Center. He didn't even do anything all that bad. He didn't hurt anybody. Not like Bo does. He's actually really nice. He just had some tough stuff going on in his life that he tried to get away from. I don't understand why he's being punished so harshly."

"I know why," Jessie said. "For the same reason we have to plan for an extra hour of travel every time we come back from visiting my aunt in Bisbee."

"Why?" I asked him.

Jessie shook his head at me. "Border patrol, Gus. They search our car and make us show proof that we're citizens. Every. Single. Time."

"My dad gets stopped a lot, too," Rossi said. "I've heard him gripe about it making him late for work."

Jessie snorted. "They probably can't even tell the difference," he said, his voice tight and angry—not at all like he usually sounded. "All they see is a brown person in a junky car."

I swallowed. What could I say to that? Nothing. There was nothing I could say.

We kept walking. "My dad was so angry when that happened. I'd never seen him so angry. The next day he went down and registered at the college for the social work program."

Rossi cleared her throat. "After he took the job at the Center, he sold his bike to pay the deposit on our apartment in Casa Grande, so that was the end of that. No more riding together. No more motorcycle club. No more powwows. It was like he stopped caring about anything, and anyone, but those boys. Then all it took was our car breaking down once, and we couldn't make our rent. After a few months, we ended up here. And the day we moved here, to this town. I gave up hope of ever going back. That day . . . that's my worst day." She stopped and looked over the map for a moment. "I miss my home. I miss my friends." She squeezed her eyes shut. "I hate it here," she added in a whisper.

We followed her quietly for a while, all of us lost in thought. I wanted to understand what Rossi and Jessie were talking about, wanted to see the world through their eyes, but I had a feeling I never could.

I looked at Rossi walking beside me, checking the map every now and then. "I'm sorry your mom died," I said.

She shrugged a little. "I can hardly remember her.

I think I was too young to fully understand what it meant. That she was really gone forever. And I hate that I can't remember her better. The only things I really remember . . ." she trailed off.

"What?" I asked.

Rossi cleared her throat. "I remember we used to play *tóka* together."

"What's that?" Matthew asked.

"It's an O'odham game." Rossi raised an eyebrow. "For girls only. Sorry, guys."

I laughed. "How do you play?"

"It's like field hockey," Rossi said. "But not. It has more meaning. I remember being the youngest girl on the field. The other women said I was too young, but my mother told them not to underestimate me. That I was deceptively strong. And there was this one older girl who kept trampling all over me. I told her to lay off, but she wouldn't stop. She was just a bully picking on someone smaller than she was. I've seen them my whole life. Finally I hit her with my *usaga* so hard she rolled in the dirt. She left me alone after that."

"What's an *usaga*?" I asked.

"It's a mesquite branch. All the playing pieces come from the desert." Rossi smiled. "And I remember the song we used to sing before a game." She hummed a few notes. "I remember how our house smelled. Like creosote oil and fresh bread and saguaro fruit jam cooking on the stove. Now my house smells like . . . like no one lives there at all." She stared at the map and swallowed. "Anyway, that's what I remember."

"I love the smell of creosote when it rains," I told her. "Sometimes I'll pick a piece of it and carry it around with me so I can sniff it every now and then. It makes me feel like it could rain." She didn't look at me—just kept staring at the map. But I saw her smile just a little bit.

"How come guys can't play *tóka*?" Matthew griped. "The girls worried they'll lose?"

Rossi's smile broadened. "They would absolutely crush you, Matthew. Kind of like I do at racing."

Jessie threw his hand over his mouth and pointed at Matthew. "Ohhhhh. She got you."

Suddenly I saw something familiar behind Jessie. "Hey, I think I've seen those rocks. They look like a snowman. And that one over there looks like a stack of tires. We've definitely been here. I think the petroglyphs are this way."

I kept looking for familiar rocks until a couple of bats flew over our heads. "Okay," Rossi said, her voice unsteady. "We must be going the right way." Then she ran ahead of us a bit. "Here!" she called. "They're here!"

"Wait, Rossi!" I cried, but it was too late. I was down, the rocks tearing the skin on my hands as I tried to brace myself. Matthew and Jessie helped me up, and we joined her at the petroglyphs, stumbling over the rocks with the limited light.

"You can't run off with the light," I told her.

"Sorry, Gus," she murmured, completely focused on the wall. She pointed at the arrow. "So we should go in this direction, I think."

We followed her for a few minutes until we made it to a dead end in a small room of the cave. "We'd better turn around," I said. "We must have missed something." Then one wall of the room caught my eye, and I stood there, shining the flashlight on it, mesmerized.

"That's really weird," Matthew said, standing beside me.

"Hey," Jessie said. "It looks like a dude." He walked toward the wall. "Like a face."

"It looks like...," Rossi said, shining the flashlight on it.

We all tilted our heads a little to the side and said in unison, "Abraham Lincoln."

"Look." I outlined it with my finger. "There's his beard, his top hat. There are even two holes where his nose is. There must be something in one of those nostrils!"

Matthew nudged Jessie forward. "Go stick your fingers in his nose."

Jessie's head shot back. "No way. You stick your fingers in Abraham Lincoln's nose."

"No, you," Matthew said. "Come on. You know you want to. Pick it."

"You pick it."

"Pick it. Pick it. Pick it," said Matthew while Jessie repeatedly told him no.

"Maybe Gus should pick it," Jessie finally said.

"I'm not tall enough to reach in there," I said. "How about you guys choose a number between one and ten?"

"One," said Matthew.

"Ten," said Jessie.

"Jessie gets to pick the nose," I said.

Jessie groaned as he hesitantly slipped his hand into the hole. He yelped and pulled it back out. "There's something in there!"

"Maybe it's a giant booger," Matthew said, laughing.

"Just reach in and pull it out," I told him.

Jessie reached in again and then quickly pulled his hand out, a dirty, holey, cowboy hat in his hands.

We all looked at one another excitedly. "Is there anything else in there?" I asked.

Jessie threw the hat down and reached his hand back into the hole. He grunted as he stretched as far as he could go. "I think so," he said. He finally pulled his arm out, a small wooden box in his hand.

"Whoa," Matthew said. Jessie ran his fingers over the initials engraved on the box—W.A.D., just like the watch. Jessie unclasped the box and opened it.

"No," I breathed.

It was empty.

"I knew it," Jessie said. "I knew we shouldn't have come here."

"We still haven't checked the other hole," I said hopefully.

Jessie handed Matthew the box and reached his arm into the other hole, his eyes clenched shut. "There's something in this one, too." He grunted as he pulled his arm out, a wadded up cloth in his hand. "It's heavy," he said as he unraveled it.

Jessie let out a huge squeaky breath as he saw what was under it: an old pistol. "Oh my gosh," he said in shaky whisper, his hands trembling.

We stepped back instinctively. "Jessie," I said as the pistol started sliding from the cloth. "Be careful. You don't want to —"

But then he dropped the gun and a loud explosion filled the cave.

THE THREE OF US COVERED OUR EARS

and ducked as Jessie screamed. Once I knew for sure I wasn't going to be hit and my ears stopped ringing enough that I could hear, I ran to Jessie.

He was jumping around howling. I grabbed at his flailing arms. "Are you okay?" I kept yelling, but he didn't hear me.

Rossi picked up the flashlight and knelt on the ground at Jessie's feet. She attempted to hold his leg while he writhed around. "Stop it!" she shouted at him. "Calm down."

Matthew and I grabbed his arms and tried to keep him steady while Rossi inspected his foot. "I shot myself, man! I shot myself!" He threw his head back and wailed in a way that made me fear he had shot off half his body.

Rossi held his foot in her lap—a tiny corner of his sneaker had exploded, and red was already spreading from the site of the explosion.

Rossi looked up at me. "I don't think it's too serious." She looked unsure. "I'm going to take your shoe off," she told Jessie.

"No!" Jessie screamed. "Don't touch it!"

She shook her head. "I don't know what to do."

"We need to get out of here," I said. "He needs a doctor."

"I can't!" Jessie wailed. "I can't walk!"

I turned to Matthew. "We'll have to help him."

"I can't walk through this cave," Jessie whimpered. "I want my ma. I want to go home."

"We're going home," I told him. "We're going back to where the pigs came from. There's got to be a way out there. It's not far." Jessie continued his whimpering and wailing. "Wasn't there anything else in the holes?" I asked him, but he was too hysterical to answer.

Without having to ask, Matthew reached in and felt both holes. He didn't need to say a thing. His face told me everything.

"This was all for nothing!" Jessie cried. "This is so

much worse than if Andy Letterman had been here! No gold! I told you guys we shouldn't come! I've shot myself for nothing!"

"You need to calm down," I told him, doing my best to forget my own crushing disappointment. We needed to focus on Jessie now. "We're getting out of here." I pulled his arm over my shoulder. "We'll help you." Matthew pulled Jessie's other arm over his shoulder. "We're your crutches."

"Rossi." She turned to me. "I'm sorry. I really thought it would be here."

"It's okay, Gus," she said. "I did, too." Her face was filled with fear. I knew what she was thinking. What if we were stuck in here? Stuck in here and now Jessie was injured. And who knew how much life was left in that flashlight. Jessie was right. This was all for nothing. I could have just killed us all.

"We'll follow you," I said.

Rossi shined the flashlight on the map. "Okay," she said. "We go this way."

Matthew and I held on to Jessie as he hopped on one foot through the cave. It was tough and slow going making it over the boulders and rocky ground and tight spaces with Jessie injured.

Rossi frequently checked the map, but before

long, our surroundings were looking different. In a bad way.

I stopped. "I don't think we've been here before."

Rossi turned in a circle, shining the flashlight all around us. "I don't think so, either. I think . . . I think I led us the wrong way." She looked at the map, and I noticed how it shook in her hand. She dropped it down by her side. "I'm sorry," she whispered, her eyes squeezed shut. "I don't know where we are on this thing."

I took a deep breath. "It's okay. We'll just go back. We must have made a wrong turn somewhere."

We turned around and went back the way we came, but after a while I realized something.

dire: dreadful, frightful, alarming

We were lost. We had no idea where we were in this cave. We had limited light and hadn't been looking for familiar landmarks like we should have been. We thought the map would guide us. We were all too scared and focused on Jessie to have noticed we were making wrong turns. We could wander here forever. And soon, we'd be in the dark.

"We need to keep moving," I said. "How big can this cave be?"

The ground under my feet was far less rocky and had turned into a sort of crackled clay. I reached down and touched a finger to it—the dirt was fine and red. I looked up at Rossi. "Do you think there used to be water here?"

"I've only seen this kind of ground in dry lake and river beds," she said. "It's silt." She looked at the map. "I think maybe we might be here." She pointed at something on the map that looked like a river. "If it used to be a river, maybe it leads outside."

We continued walking along the crackled ground, hoping it led somewhere, anywhere.

"Maybe we're going deeper into the ground." Matthew breathed heavily and his voice trembled. "Maybe we'll get too close to the earth's core and it will get too hot and it will burn us to death."

Jessie made scared, wheezing sounds beside me.

"It's not hot," I said. "We're not going to the earth's core. And that's not helping." I stood there a moment. "Actually . . . I feel a slight breeze."

"You're crazy, Gus," Jessie cried. "You've lost your mind."

I let go of Jessie and walked to Rossi. I grabbed the flashlight from her and pointed it at her head. It flickered, and we all gasped.

I tried to focus on Rossi's hair. I remembered how it had blown back from her face when she'd first opened the hole in the mine wall. A few thin strands of hair lightly lifted and blew in the direction we had come from.

"I think your Indian sense was leading us in the right direction," I said.

"How can you joke at a time like this?" Jessie said, but Rossi just stared at me.

She licked her finger and held it up. "I feel it."

Except for the sounds of Matthew's heavy breathing and Jessie's whimpers, we walked quietly in the direction of the breeze.

And then Rossi stopped abruptly in front of us. I let go of Jessie and walked up beside her. She pointed the flashlight straight ahead. "Oh. No," she said.

"What is it?" Matthew asked. He walked up next to us, Jessie hobbling by his side. "Shoot," Matthew whispered.

I swallowed, and, despite the extreme humidity in the room, my throat felt like the dried up skeleton of a saguaro cactus. We had reached the big, dark, shaded area.

"We're all going to die," Jessie said.

9:00 AM

I SHINED THE FLASHLIGHT ACROSS THE
glassy blackness of the large lake in front of us. The
light flickered, and I smacked it. I picked up a pebble
and tossed it. It made a loud echoing plop, and the
black sheet rippled like it was made of satin. I turned
the flashlight off.

A moment later, we were in darkness. The ceiling
came down very low over the center of the lake, and I
knelt to see under it. "Do you guys see that?"

I waited a little while as our eyes adjusted to the dark.

"I see it," Rossi said, crouching down beside me.

"What?" Jessie asked. "What do you see?"

"Light," Rossi said.

"Where?" Matthew asked.

"On the other side of the lake," Rossi said. "You

have to get down to see all the way across because the ceiling is so low toward the middle."

I turned the flashlight back on. It flickered again. I saw that Rossi's eyes were wide with fear. "Can everyone swim?" I asked.

"I can," Jessie said, leaning against Matthew for support. "Sometimes we swim at the pool in Casa Grande. But I don't think I can right now because of my foot."

"I can," Matthew said. "A little anyway. Jacob used to have a pool at his trailer before it broke and flooded his yard a few years ago. The pool, I mean, not the trailer. I think his dad built it out of tarps and pipes or something crazy like that. You learn how to swim pretty quickly when Bo is there to dunk you when you're not paying attention. It's been a couple of years, though. I think I can remember. I mean, I hope I can. We played Marco Polo a lot—you say Marco and the others are supposed to say Polo. You have your eyes closed so it's like being in the dark. So I think I can."

prattle: gab; babble

We were all nervous. I only knew how to swim (barely) from before my dad ditched me. He once did a big window job at a hotel in Reno. We snuck in a few times to use the pool since he had access, even though he wasn't supposed to do that. We ended up getting kicked out by security on our fourth trip, but I had learned to doggy-paddle by then. It had been a long time, though. "I guess you probably don't forget how," I said to Matthew. "You think?"

Matthew nodded. "Maybe it's not even very deep. Maybe we can walk across."

"Rossi?" I said.

"I'll do it."

"Have you ever been swimming?" I asked her, as she hadn't actually answered the question.

She didn't look at me. "I'll make it across."

I didn't want to question her further. But I was scared. "What about your helmet? You can't swim while holding your helmet."

Rossi gripped it protectively to her chest. She shook her head. "I can't leave it behind, Gus. I won't be able to get another one."

"I'll swim with it," I said. "I can hold it above the water."

"What about the flashlight?" Jessie asked.

"I'll hold them both. I'll hold the flashlight in my mouth."

"I'll hold the flashlight," Matthew said.

"You have to carry Jessie," I said. "There's no way."

"For goodness sake," Jessie cried. "I can at least carry the flashlight."

"You have to hold on to Matthew."

"Geez, Gus. You must think I'm totally incapable. I think I can hold on to Matthew and carry that tiny flashlight at the same time."

I handed him the helmet. "Fine, then. Put this on your head. But I'm holding the flashlight so I can be out front. I want to make sure there's nothing dangerous in the water."

Jessie's eyes became huge. "Like a crocodile," he whispered.

"No, I was thinking more like a jagged rock. Here." I handed him the pocket watch. "Try to keep this out of the water."

"What about our shoes?" Matthew said. "It's hard to swim with shoes."

"How will we ever walk back to town without them?" I said. "The ground will burn the skin off the bottom of our feet after two steps."

"Plus cactus," Jessie said.

"Our feet will melt off before we ever feel any cactus."

I sighed. "Maybe we should go back and try to find the javelina way."

Rossi shook her head. "We could get lost again and then not be able to find our way back *here*. And the flashlight doesn't have much life left. We'd be lost in the dark." I shivered. I couldn't think of anything worse than being lost in the pitch blackness, having to feel our way through the cave, not knowing what kind of animals we might run into, Jessie unable to walk. "There's an opening over there. We have to try."

I took a deep breath. "No more time to stand around talking about it then."

I pointed the flashlight straight ahead and stepped down into the inky water. I was surprised at how warm it was, but I shouldn't have been—there was no cool water in Nowhere. I walked slowly, hoping it stayed as shallow as it was. My feet sunk in a little with each step, almost like I was walking in peanut butter, and I worried my shoes would get sucked off. Suddenly I stepped on some kind of stick. Odd. There weren't any trees or bushes in the cave. I aimed the flashlight at it.

My hands trembled as I peered into the water. "What is it?" Matthew said, now standing beside me, the water already up to my knees but only midway up his shins. "It's just a white stick, right?" His voice shook.

"It looks like a bone, man!" Jessie cried from underneath the helmet.

Rossi splashed through the water until she was beside us. She reached down and loosened the bone from the mud. She pulled it from the water. "It is."

"Is it from an animal?" Matthew asked.

Rossi and I looked at each other—the only animal this bone came from was the kind that shot their partner, hid in mines, set off explosives, and never came back out.

I shined the flashlight into the water all around us—more bones. And then . . .

"No way," Matthew whispered.

Once more Rossi reached down. "Don't touch it!" Jessie cried.

She ignored him and lifted the skull out of the water. She raised it to the level of her face, like she was saying hello. Then she turned it around so it faced Matthew. "Say hello to your great-grandfather."

Matthew took a step back in the water. "We don't know that's my great-grandfather."

I walked around, kicking at the muddy ground, loosening more bones. Something hard and shiny emerged from the mud. I rinsed it off and lifted it out of the water. It was a metal flask with something engraved on it.

"W.A.D.," Rossi whispered. She looked at Matthew. "I guess we do know."

"Your great-grandfather sure liked to put his name on stuff," I told Matthew.

"Yeah, he was probably worried about people stealing his things," he retorted.

I ignored Matthew as I continued kicking at the mud. And then my foot hit a soft, dark clump of something. I lifted it and held it out, mud dripping into the water.

"Great," Jessie said. "Now Gus found a big clump of mud. Can we please stop wasting time and get out of here before I get gangrene or something?"

"Hold on," I whispered. It wasn't just a clump of mud. I rinsed it off as well as I could in the water and then held it back up. "It's a leather pouch." I felt around it until I found two strings.

"Open it, Gus," Rossi said.

I loosened the tie and pulled it open. The three of them huddled around me in the water as I shined the dimming flashlight inside.

"It's filled with mud," Matthew said.

Shaking my head, I reached in and felt around. I pulled out a small pebble. I rinsed if off in the water then held it back up. It flashed yellow in the light of the flashlight. "It's gold."

The three of them gasped. "How much is in there?" Matthew asked.

"I can't tell since it's all filled with mud," I said.

We made our way back to the dry ground where we'd entered the lake, and I dumped the bag out. We sifted through the mud, rinsing the pieces of gold off in the water and laying them out.

I looked at Rossi. "I can't believe it."

Rossi pursed her lips. "I guess that settles the question once and for all of who stole the gold. But why did your great-grandfather have that pocket watch, Gus?"

"Maybe William Dufort dropped it," Jessie said. "And when he couldn't find it, he thought José had taken it, and he stole the gold as revenge."

"So this means my great-grandfather really was a backstabbing thief?" Matthew said. He glowered at the gold. "That sucks."

"Who cares?" I said to Matthew. "What he did way back then has nothing to do with who you are now."

"No," Rossi said, staring at me. "It doesn't." She smiled. "That's good advice, Gus."

I felt my cheeks grow hot, and I was glad for once that it was so dark in the cave.

"So why was that other stuff in Abraham Lincoln's nose?" Jessie asked.

I thought about this a moment. "How about this?" I said.

hypothesis: a proposed explanation based on limited evidence

"William Dufort knew all about the cave, even made that map. He probably used A.L.'s nose as a hiding place for things. He must have scratched that arrow onto the rock so he would be able to find his way back there. But that night, or maybe even some time before, he dropped his watch and lost the map, which my great-grandpa found. Without it, and with being shot and all, maybe he couldn't find his way around and ended up here, where he tried to cross the lake."

"And he drowned," Rossi said. "He probably couldn't swim."

"Or he just fell over dead from blood loss," I said.

"Then your drunk grandfather got bitten by a rattlesnake on his way home and died in the desert," Matthew added.

"Pretty much," I agreed.

"Interesting theory," Rossi said.

"So whose is it?" Jessie asked. "Who does the gold belong to then?"

We were all quiet for a moment.

"I don't want the gold," Rossi spoke up. "Just a piece for Bo if that's okay."

"I don't want any, either," Matthew said. "I shouldn't get any."

"Don't say that," Jessie said. "We're all in this together. We'll split it up evenly."

Matthew stared at Jessie. "Are you sure?"

Jessie nodded. "We found it together. Like Gus said, what happened back then has nothing to do with us now."

Matthew beamed at Jessie. "Thanks, man."

We all stared down at the gold pieces. "So how much do you think it's worth?" Jessie asked.

I gathered the gold up and stuck it back in the leather pouch, feeling its weight. "I don't know. This is maybe a pound. Maybe more. Hard to say. Mayor Handsome said an ounce goes for a few hundred dollars. So multiply that by sixteen."

"Why sixteen?" Matthew asked.

We all looked at him. "Because there are sixteen ounces in a pound," I said.

He nodded. "Oh. Good call."

"We need to decide which piece we'll give to Bo before we can split it up," I said. "And it shouldn't be anything too small or he might not agree to trade."

"Or too big," said Matthew.

"Something sort of medium then," said Jessie.

I pulled a piece out of the pouch, but they all mumbled that it was too big. Then I pulled another piece out, and they all agreed it was too big again. No one seemed to think any piece I pulled out was too small.

"I'm just going to give him the next piece I pull out," I told them. They all grumbled when they saw the size of it. "Too late," I said, sticking it into my pocket. "That one's for Bo." I tied up the bag as well as I could and put it in my backpack.

"How will we divide it up?" Matthew asked.

"We'll have to go into the city and sell it somehow," I said. "Then we can split the money. But we have to promise right now. We have to promise we won't tell anyone about what we found. If Bo finds out, he'll take it from us." I stared at Matthew.

"I promise," Matthew said, clearly annoyed I was

singling him out. Then in a less annoyed tone: "Gus, really, I promise."

"I promise," said Jessie.

"Me, too," said Rossi.

"I do, too," I said. "And we can't tell anyone about the cave, either."

"Why?" Matthew asked.

I looked at Rossi. "To protect it. If people find out about it, what do you think they'll do?"

"Trash it," said Rossi.

"Right," I said. "Dump their trash, graffiti the walls, steal whatever they can bust out of here. This place is special. The only way to keep it like that is to keep it secret."

The others nodded in agreement. "Okay," Matthew said. "No telling about the cave." His eyes twinkled in the dim light. "Do you think there will be enough gold to go to Disneyland?"

"Well," I said. "At a pound, that's maybe five thousand dollars. That would be over a thousand dollars apiece. So yeah, I think so."

"A thousand dollars," Matthew whispered. "I'll be rich."

"Yeah, maybe you can finally ride Pirates of the Caribbean" I told him. Then I looked at Rossi. "And maybe you can visit home now. See your friends."

She nodded and smiled. "I see one right now."

My cheeks burned as I smiled back at her. The flashlight flickered. "We'd really better get moving."

The four of us stepped back into the water and started making our way across the lake. Suddenly Rossi jumped and gave a small shriek, splashing water around her.

"What?" I asked.

She grabbed the flashlight from me and aimed it into the water. "It felt like something touched my leg."

"There's creatures in here!" Jessie screamed. He climbed up on Matthew's back so his feet were out of the water.

"Geez. You're heavy, man." But Matthew let him stay up there.

"Calm down," I said, though I was feeling on the verge of panic myself. I stared into the water until I saw them.

"What are they?" Jessie's voice quaked.

"Crawdads?" I asked Rossi.

She nodded. "I think so. Or some strange mutant albino shrimp of some kind."

"They're mutants!" Jessie cried. "Will they pinch us?"

I shrugged. "I don't know, but we need to get moving. This flashlight is almost dead."

I turned and trudged through the water—ancient cave water filled with mutant albino shrimp and the bones of a nearly one-hundred-year-old dead French guy. The situation could have been creepier, though. There could have been, like, clowns in the water.

I walked slowly, feeling each step carefully, shining the flashlight all around. Every now and then I would step on something I didn't even want to know about. When the water reached my neck and the ceiling was low enough that I could touch it, I nervously started calling out, "Marco."

The three of them behind me would respond, "Polo." I always made sure I heard three voices.

When we were about thirty feet from the other side, I could barely touch the bottom on tip-toe and still keep my face above water. "It's too deep," I called to them, straining to keep my mouth out of the water. I turned around—they were all pretty close behind me, Rossi trailing the two guys. "We'll have to swim, but only for a little while, I think."

"Let's do it," Matthew said, Jessie clinging to his back.

I turned around, lifted my feet, held the flashlight in the air, and kicked with all my might. It's tough to swim with shoes on. Even tougher when you can't use both hands. Even tougher when there's a ceiling right over your head, making you feel closet-tropic. "Marco," I called out breathlessly.

"Polo," I heard the three call.

When the effort became too much, I had to stick the flashlight in my mouth so I could use both hands to doggy paddle. I was completely focused on making it to the other side at this point. I wasn't thinking about anything, or anyone, else. It was all I could do to muster the strength to make it across.

I finally reached the dry ledge and threw the flashlight on it. I pulled myself up, using every last bit of strength in me, and rolled onto the dry floor of the cave. I took a couple of deep breaths then jumped up and grabbed the flashlight, which was barely functioning at this point. I looked for the others.

Matthew was almost to the ledge—still carrying Jessie—his face contorted into a grimace from the effort. I crouched down so I could see under the ceiling. But there was no one behind them.

"Rossi!" I screamed. My voice echoed through the cave, saying her name a hundred times.

Matthew helped Jessie to the ledge and the two

of them turned their heads sharply, searching for her. "Rossi!" I screamed again. No answer.

In this type of situation, a person often dives into the water dramatically to save someone. However, I wasn't much for theatrics. I also wasn't much for killing myself by smashing my head into some hidden boulder or stalagmite under the water. That wouldn't help Rossi at all.

So I did the sensible and unimpressive thing and jumped into the water feet first. I swam back the way we'd come, ducking under the dark water and feeling everywhere. I had been completely spent just seconds ago, feeling like I couldn't possibly swim another inch. Now I felt like I could cross an ocean if I needed to.

Matthew was up on the ledge, shining the flashlight into the water for me. Still, I could barely see.

There was only one thought in my head—find her. I dove over and over again, spinning my hands around, feeling the water.

Then I grasped it—hair. It tangled in my fingers. I gripped it as hard as I could and yanked. When I felt her arm, I pulled her up with all my might. I found strength I didn't know I had as I lifted her face out of the water and swam back to the ledge.

Jessie was still clinging to the side, whimpering, "Rossi, please be okay. Please be okay."

Matthew reached out both hands and dragged her onto the ledge. Then I pulled myself up and fell to my knees over her. She wasn't breathing.

10:00 AM

NOWHERE ELEMENTARY SUCKED. THAT

was for sure. And our health class was just as pathetic as everything else. We had exactly one ancient, creepy, dirty dummy that had tasted the chapped lips of a thousand scruffy Nowhere children for the whole school to practice CPR on. That meant a lot of waiting around while kids pretended to French kiss it, lick its nose, poke its rubber breasts, massage its head— pretty much everything you can imagine *except* give it CPR.

When it was my one-and-only turn, being the total geek that I am, I actually performed CPR on the dummy. This was met with cries of "Teacher's pet!" and "Goody-goody!"

I felt for the end of Rossi's breastbone. I placed

two fingers at the tip and pressed the heel of my hand above that. I remembered Mr. Johnson telling us to use a lot of pressure and to not worry about breaking the person's ribs. Better to break her ribs than for her to . . .

As I pressed into her chest with all the strength in me, I heard Jessie crying from the water, "Don't die, Rossi. Don't die."

Die. Rossi could die.

My world sucked pretty bad. Take Rossi out of it, and the level of suckness was unimaginable.

Matthew hovered over me as the flashlight burned out in his hands. I tilted Rossi's head back and pinched her nose with my fingers. I placed my mouth over hers and blew into it. I watched her chest in the faint light of the nearby opening. It rose and fell with every breath. Then I did more chest compressions. I tilted her head back once more, pinched her nose, and breathed into her.

Just as Rossi had sworn she would never watch Bo hurt me again, I swore to myself I would not let her die. She couldn't die now. Not now. We had the gold. We were going to get her bike back. She was going to win. She was going to go to Breaker Bradley's. She would find a sponsor. She would get to Baja, and do all one thousand miles. Her life was not going to end down here. Not at thirteen years old. Not in this cave. Not in this darkness. Not like this.

I thought of her on the ledge under the full moon, telling me she hoped she died on her bike. Telling me she didn't care whether she was here or not. Well, I cared. I cared whether she was here or not. And I cared enough for the both of us.

Rossi coughed and gagged. I pushed her onto her side and she threw up a gallon of water. Matthew fell to his knees beside me. He exhaled like he had been holding his breath.

Rossi rolled onto her back, gasping for air. When her breathing finally evened out, I helped her into a sitting position. She fell back against me. "I told you I'd make it," she said in a hoarse whisper.

"Gus saved your life, Rossi." Matthew wiped at his nose. "You almost died."

I couldn't see her face. She didn't speak.

"Could someone please help me out of the water?" Jessie cried from under the helmet. "I think a shrimp is trying to eat my exploded foot. And it hurts. Bad."

Matthew hauled him up onto the ledge, and he cried out in pain as his foot grazed the side. He crawled on all fours to Rossi, still holding the pocket watch in his hand. "Are you okay?"

She nodded slightly. "I just need a minute. To catch my breath."

Matthew took a few shaky breaths as he composed himself. Then he walked over to where the light was coming out of the ceiling, hunched down so he didn't hit his head, and looked up. "There's a hole up there. But it's going to be hard to get to. We'll have to push ourselves up using the sides. And it looks like there are bushes growing over it. Hopefully there's no cactus." Matthew scowled. "I don't know how we'll get Jessie up, since he can't use his foot. And Rossi—"

"I'll make it," she said. "I'll be okay."

"Yeah, I've heard that before," said Matthew.

"You guys can come back for me," said Jessie.

"No," Matthew said. "We're not leaving you here in the dark. We get out of here together. We're not leaving anyone behind."

I left Rossi to check out the hole. "I think we can climb up." I glanced at the guys. "Anyone been rock climbing?" They shook their heads. "With someone at the top to help pull and someone down here to help push him up, I think we can get Jessie up without him having to use his foot too much."

"Who goes first then?" Matthew asked.

"You should," I said. "You're the strongest. You can

pull Jessie up, and Rossi and I can try to boost him up as far as possible. You okay with that?" I asked Jessie.

He looked scared. "I guess I have to be."

I crouched down so Matthew could climb on my back and get a grip inside the hole. "I can't pull myself up," he said. "I need to get higher."

Rossi crawled over to us and crouched down. Matthew stepped up on her and then climbed onto my shoulders. He was incredibly heavy, and I worried I would fall over, but then Rossi said, "You're strong, Gus," and I felt like she infused me with muscle power I didn't know I had.

I stood up tall with Matthew on my shoulders. "I'm sorry, Gus," he said as he pulled himself up and stepped on my head. I resisted the urge to grunt and groan.

We watched him climb up the hole, keeping himself from falling by pushing against one side with his legs, his back against the other side. He shimmied up that way and disappeared above us.

Then his head reappeared in the opening. "I'm out!" he called.

We cheered, and Rossi hugged me.

"The good news," Matthew said, "is these bushes moved easily, like they just blew into the hole."

I frowned. "Is there bad news?"

Matthew nodded. "I seem to be at the bottom of some kind of pit."

Jessie groaned. "We'll never get out."

"Don't worry," I told Jessie. "At least we'll be outside."

"Yeah, so the sun can cook us to death," he whined.

Rossi opened my backpack from behind and pulled out the empty pickle jar, miraculously still intact. Then she knelt down and filled it with lake water.

"Uh, that water will probably give us the plague or something," Jessie said.

Probably not the plague, but definitely the trots.

"I know," she said.

"We don't know how far we'll have to walk when we get out," I said. "It won't take long for the heat to kill us. We'll only drink if we absolutely have to."

Rossi and I worked together to lift Jessie into the hole above us. He kept crying out in pain at every motion we made, and I rolled my eyes at Rossi.

Matthew reached down to try to help pull him up, but there was no way we could lift him high enough, even though he was on our shoulders. "You're going to have to climb a little bit," I told him.

"I can't," Jessie cried.

"Yes, you can!" I ordered him. "Man up, Jesus!"

Jessie was quiet, obviously startled at my sudden authoritarian approach. "You can do it," I told him again.

He took a deep breath, gripped the sides of the hole, jumped off of our shoulders and pushed his feet against the wall. He cried out in pain, and I felt bad about having yelled at him.

I looked up at Matthew. He was focused on Jessie. "You can do it," he told him. "You'll get through it, Jessie." It was the first time Matthew had ever called him that.

Finally, he reached a point where Matthew could grab him and help pull him up. And then he was gone. Rossi looked at me. "Gus, you go."

I shook my head. "No way."

"How are you going to get up without help?"

I shrugged. "I'll figure something out. And if I don't, you guys can come back and get me after the race."

She shook her head. "No, I want you there." She touched my shredded pants and shirt. Then she looked down at her own clothing. "Like Rapunzel."

"You're going to use your hair to pull me up?"

"No, but that's the idea. We need something to make a rope."

"Our clothes?"

She nodded. Then I boosted her up into the hole. She threw her helmet up to Matthew and pushed her feet against the side, but she didn't move. After a few seconds, she dropped out of the hole. I managed to catch her but fell back. I kept her from hitting the ground with my body.

She shook her head. "I'm so sorry, Gus. I got dizzy."

"You've been through a lot. Maybe we should wait so you can rest longer. I mean, you just nearly drowned."

"No." She pushed herself up. "There's no time for that." She stood and swayed a little. I held on to her until she was steady. Then I helped boost her back up into the hole. I stood underneath her in case she fell again, but I could see the determination on her face as she pushed herself up the hole. She finally reached Matthew and he pulled her up.

I listened while she argued with Matthew and Jessie. They whined and groaned and finally relented. And then, about five minutes later, a rope made out of boys' ripped-up jeans and T-shirts floated down to me.

I jumped and gripped it. I heard Matthew grunt as he tried to hold my weight. I climbed with all my might. We'd never done rope climbing in school, but I found it wasn't as hard as I'd expected—I didn't have a whole lot of weight to pull up.

Before long, I was completely in the hole and able to use the walls to rappel myself up as the others had.

I climbed out of it, breathing heavily from the effort. I shielded my eyes from the blinding sunlight and tried to make out our situation. Matthew was in his underpants, but Jessie still had his jeans on—I guessed because it was too painful for him to remove his shoes. Rossi was sitting on the ground, facing the wall of the deep pit we were in like she had been put in timeout.

We quickly unraveled the rope, and the guys got dressed. When they had all their clothes on, Rossi was finally free to turn around. Jessie raised his spindly arms and flexed them. "Sorry you missed the ultimate display of macho manliness, Rossi."

She turned in a circle, inspecting the hole around us. "Yes, I am, too." She looked at me. "You know, Gus, I think you look taller."

I stood up straight. The truth was I *felt* taller, like I had grown three inches in that cave. Maybe I'd finally hit that elusive growth spurt everyone else seemed to have gone through except me.

Then we faced the next obstacle in the course—getting out of the pit.

"What is this, some kind of sinkhole?" I said.

Rossi nodded. "We'll have to climb somehow."

I checked the pocket watch. "It's almost eleven already."

Rossi's face sunk. "We'll never make it."

"Yes, we will," Matthew insisted. He grabbed at a rock sticking out of the side of the sinkhole and attempted to pull himself up. The rock broke free of the wall, and he tumbled to the ground.

"You're too heavy," I told him. "I think I have to be the one to climb. Then I'll bring help back for you guys."

Rossi shook her head. "That's going to take too long. There's no way."

"I can do it," I told her. "I'll be fast."

I found another rock sticking out of the side of the wall and attempted to climb. I stepped on another rock that was only about six inches off the ground. I looked up, straining to reach a stick higher above.

"Gus," Rossi said.

"Shhh," I told her. "I'm trying to concentrate."

"Hey, Gus," Jessie said.

"You guys," I snapped. "I have to focus." If only I could somehow get my foot up on the rock I was gripping with my hand, then I could reach this root protruding several feet above. I'd probably have to dig out some kind of foothold. Maybe I could use one the of the rocks like a pick or make a spear out of—

"Gus!" Rossi cried.

I dropped down the six inches of progress I'd made and whipped around. "What?"

"Look!" she said, pointing at a rope ladder that had rolled down the other side of the sinkhole.

Mayor Handsome popped his head over the side. "Yoo-hoo! Vhat you doing down dere?"

"Mayor Handsome!" I called. "We need help!"

"Yep. I see dat. Climb up."

The four of us looked at one another and laughed. We were getting out. We were getting Rossi to the race. And for the first time in my life, I was excited to get back to Nowhere.

"Don't forget." I stuck my hand out. "Promise." The others placed their hands on mine.

Then we climbed up Mayor Handsome's rope ladder. Jessie even made it without too much complaining.

When I got to the top of the sinkhole, I gazed around, trying to make sense of where we were. I saw Mayor Handsome's quad nearby.

"What are you doing out here?" I asked him, taking note of the supplies fastened to the four wheeler—mostly different kinds of netting.

Mayor Handsome shrugged. "Just a little shrimp fishing before dee race today."

I gaped at him. "You get your shrimp out of that lake? Wait, you *know* about that lake?"

There were different levels of disgust on everyone's faces. Rossi looked fairly horrified, whereas Matthew looked only slightly appalled but also very amused. Jessie, on the other hand, looked like he had just seen a mutant albino shrimp the size of a cow burst up out of the ground.

Jessie shrieked, and might have even fallen over if Matthew hadn't been supporting him. "You sell my mom mutant albino dead man cave shrimp! My mom makes mutant albino dead man cave shrimp tacos!" He wheezed like he couldn't get enough air.

Unfortunately, I had also indulged a time or two in Mrs. Navarro's mutant albino dead man cave shrimp tacos. I could tell from the look on Rossi's face that she'd eaten them as well. I mean, they were pretty tasty and I hadn't died or anything. But still.

"What are you laughing about?" Jessie yelled at Matthew.

"Mayor Handsome," Rossi said. "You do realize you're selling shrimp you got out of a lake that has a dead body in it?"

Mayor Handsome waved a dismissive hand. "*Pfft*. Dere all kinds of dead bodies in dee ocean, and everybody still eating crab legs."

Rossi stared at him. "*So* not the same thing."

"Vhat you kids doing out here anyvay?" Mayor Handsome adjusted his denim cut-offs—they were incredibly short and required a lot of adjusting. "Vhat you kids doing in dee cave? Your parents know you out here?"

We all glanced at one another. We hadn't worked out a story to tell anyone. Did we need to work out a story? We all kind of shrugged.

"We won't tell if you won't," I said.

Mayor Handsome shook his head. "Not my business." He looked at his watch then at Rossi. "Vhy you not getting ready for dee race?"

Rossi stepped forward. "Mayor Handsome, how far is it back to town?"

"Mile. Mile and a half."

"Can you fit us on your quad?"

He removed his giant cowboy hat and scratched at his perfectly coifed hair. He frowned. "I fit maybe one."

Rossi looked at me, then at Jessie and Matthew. "Go, Rossi," Jessie said. "You need to get your bike and get to the race."

"No." Rossi turned to Mayor Handsome. "Jessie needs to get to a doctor. Can you drive him back?"

Mayor Handsome nodded. "Of course. You kids have vater?"

We all shook our heads—at least not water that wouldn't make us seriously ill.

Mayor handsome clucked his tongue and pulled a gallon milk container filled with water off his quad. Matthew helped Jessie limp over and onto the four wheeler.

"*Pew!*" Mayor Handsome cried out. "You stink, Jessie!"

"Yeah, that's not all dirt on his clothes," Matthew said.

"I'm not the only one covered in poo," Jessie muttered. "At least I don't also have Twinkie filling all over me."

Mayor Handsome handed the jug to Rossi. "You kids die valking back to town vidout vater."

Rossi looked at me, her eyes filled with urgency. I took a deep breath. "More like running."

WE FOLLOWED A LARGE WASH FROM

where we were, as Mayor Handsome had instructed. And run we did . . . for about ten seconds before we totally gassed out from the overwhelming heat and exhaustion. We had to stop a couple of times for Rossi to catch her breath, and I worried about her making it.

We tried to take our minds off of our misery by making jokes. "This is how Mrs. Lopez speed-walks through town." Matthew pumped his arms up and down over his head and shook his butt in an embarrassingly exaggerated way.

"No, like this." I handed the jug of water to Matthew, stuck my butt out, and wiggled my hips while pretending to lift small weights with my arms. The ninety-year-old

woman was a great source of entertainment for everyone as she exercised her way through town every day.
She was probably the only person in Nowhere who exercised. Which was probably why she was the oldest.

Even Rossi got into it, impersonating the prancing
exercises of Mrs. Lopez as we moved as quickly as we
dared in the heat. We took turns passing the helmet
and jug around and taking large, gasping gulps as we
speed-walked. We used the lake water to dump on our
heads and shirts. The drinking water was gone before
we reached town, but I could see the Nowhere Market
and Ostrich Farm as we made one last turn around the
mountain, the ostriches lounging in the shaded part
of their enclosure, hiding from the heat of the day. As
though anyone could hide from it.

We walked quietly the last hundred yards or so, too
tired and hot to joke anymore. I'd never felt such an
overwhelming need to lie down. And I think I would
have given all my gold to have a cold shower right
then—a genuinely cold shower.

As we walked around from behind the store and
made our way onto the lumpy, cracked blacktop of
Nowhere's only paved road, we ran right into Bo.

"What the heck happened to you guys?" He sat on
his dirt bike in the middle of the street. Jacob Asher

sat on his own bike next to him. They were slurping at big, melting Popsicles. I hoped Bo was enjoying the last free Popsicle he would ever have.

"Did you hear what I said?" Bo barked, red Popsicle juice bursting from his mouth. The juice dripped down his chin, making him look like a vampire—a mean, ugly middle school vampire who preyed on anyone he suspected was smarter than a kindergartener.

The three of us glanced at one another. "We went into the mine," I said. "Just like our deal."

"Did it cave in on you or something?" Bo said, and he and Jacob laughed.

"No. We just worked really hard to get you what you wanted."

Bo's face was incredulous. "You actually found gold?"

I nodded. "Yep."

"So where is it?" Bo smirked and held out his hand. "Where's my gold?"

I reached into my pocket and pulled out the piece we had agreed to give him. I walked to him and slapped it into his hand. "Here. Now give us Loretta."

Bo turned the gold over in his hand, his smirk gone. "Is this for real?" he asked Matthew. "He found this in the mine?"

"Yeah," Matthew said. "It's for real. I saw him find it."

Bo grinned. "I bet he found more, too, if he found this piece."

"I didn't," I insisted. "That's all there is."

"Well, that's too bad." Bo pocketed the gold. "Because the price for Loretta went up overnight. She now costs two pieces of gold."

"You're such a liar," Rossi said through gritted teeth. "Gus went into the mine and did what you said. You can't renege on your deal."

renege: go back on a promise or contract

"I can renege on whatever I want, Rossi," Bo said. "I'll renege all up in your face. I'll renege all over this town. And don't forget it."

My heart thumped with rage. I wanted to kill Bo. Before I had a chance to act on it, Matthew said, "You're right, Bo. Gus is lying. He has more."

I looked at him in shock. "Matthew, no."

Matthew glared at me as he went and stood by Bo, his arms crossed. "He's totally lying. There's a lot more. He just doesn't want to give it up."

Rossi stormed forward and pushed Matthew so hard he flew back onto the lumpy asphalt on his butt. "You jerk!" she cried. "We all promised!"

Matthew stood up and angrily rubbed at his backside. "You shut up, Rossi." He turned to Bo. "We found a bag of treasure in there. Buried in the dirt."

I shook my head at Matthew. I couldn't believe he would turn on us so quickly.

Matthew glared back at me. "That's right. Gus has treasure. And before we came here he stopped at home and hid it in his trailer." Matthew turned to Bo. "Jewels. A whole bag of them. They're worth a lot more than gold, too, I bet."

Rossi glanced at me, confusion on her face. Then she turned back to Matthew. "You jerk," she muttered.

Matthew stared at her. "I bet he'll trade Loretta for that bag of jewels. Won't you, Bo?"

"Sure. If they're real."

"Oh, they're real," Matthew said. "You'd better bring Loretta to Gus's trailer so they don't try to go back on their deal."

"I'll bring her. But you better make sure all the jewels are there."

"Don't worry," Matthew said. "I counted them. There are seventeen." He raised his eyebrows at me, and I nodded slightly. "Yeah," Matthew said more confidently this time. "Seventeen."

Renewed with energy and adrenaline, Rossi and I ran across town to my trailer. We snuck in my bedroom window. While Rossi waited, I opened my bedroom door to peek out and see if my grandma was there. She was sitting in her chair watching TV.

"Hey, Grandma," I called.

She didn't look at me—there was a pretty intense brawl happening on the screen. "I thought you were gonna sleep all day. You okay?"

"I still don't feel too well," I said.

"Well, you better just keep on resting so you're all ready for school tomorrow."

"Will do." I shut the door and turned to my table. I opened it and pulled out the bag of jewels. The brown bag they were in had a cheesy Pirates of the Caribbean logo on it, so we dumped the gold into the Pirates bag and put the jewels in the old leather bag we'd found in the cave. I put the bag of gold in my side table, then Rossi and I jumped back out of my window.

We stood there, waiting for them to show up. After a couple of minutes, we saw three dirt bikes coming up the road—Bo on his bike, Matthew on his, and Jacob on Loretta.

The three of them pulled up to us and removed their helmets and goggles.

I squinted at Bo. "Give me your word. No going back this time. We have too many witnesses."

Bo grinned. "Of course. You give me the jewels; I give you Loretta."

I glanced at Rossi. She nodded. I walked to Bo and handed him the bag, which he immediately dumped into his palm. I knew if he inspected them too closely or bit one, or really just suddenly grew a few extra brain cells, he would realize they were totally fake. "They're all there," I said, trying to distract him. "All seventeen."

Matthew must have had the same idea because he said, "Just give them Loretta and let's get out of here, Bo. We need to get to the race."

Bo shrugged. "A deal's a deal." He walked Loretta slowly to Rossi. I watched him warily, still skeptical about him keeping his end of the bargain.

perfidious: deceitful and untrustworthy

When he was about ten feet away, Bo whipped out a pocket knife, and, before any of us could stop him, he plunged it into one of Loretta's tires.

Rossi lunged at him, but she was too late—he got the other tire, too.

"What are you doing?" Matthew screamed. "You made a deal."

Bo seemed confused at Matthew's outburst. "What? They gave me the jewels; I gave her Loretta. What do you care anyway?" He snorted. "You made friends with these losers last night, didn't you?" Bo walked to within about one inch of Matthew. "You're friends with this girl?"

Matthew stood up tall and didn't move. "You're no one's friend, Bo."

Bo laughed heartily right in Matthew's face. Then he turned to Rossi. "Good luck at the race today." He jumped back on his bike and peeled off, dirt spraying everywhere.

Jacob stood there watching Rossi as she sat on the ground next to Loretta. He looked up at me and Matthew. "Sorry," he mumbled. Then he turned and ran off.

Rossi was on her knees, inspecting the damage to her tires. She looked totally defeated. I opened the pocket watch and checked the time. It was nearly twelve. "We'll figure it out, Rossi." I refused to believe that after everything we had gone through, this was how it would all end.

She shook her head. Most of her ponytail had

come loose again, and her long dark hair obscured her face—a mess of tangles and sweat and cave dirt and lake water. "There's no way, Gus. It's impossible now."

Matthew stood over her. "I'm sorry, Rossi."

She stared at the ground. "I know you are. It's not your fault."

Then Matthew burst out, "What a bunch of garbage!" He threw his arms around like he wanted to hit something, but there was nothing to hit except sweltering, hazy air. "I can't believe that guy."

"What can't you believe?" I said. "This is who you've been hanging out with for the last four years. Don't you know who he is?"

Matthew batted at the air a few more times, cursing and huffing. Then he twisted his hands together. He looked down at Rossi. He looked at me. He looked back down at Rossi. He stopped twisting his hands. "You can use my bike, Rossi."

She peered up at him with squinted eyes. "What?"

"You can use my bike."

She shook her head. "I can't do that."

"Yes, you can. You're going to."

"But how will you race?" she asked.

Matthew shrugged. "I won't."

"I can't do that to you."

Matthew got down on the ground with her. "You beat me every single week anyway. And you'd have beaten me today. And you're the only one who can beat Bo."

Rossi shook her head again. "I can't win without my bike."

I stepped forward. "Rossi," I said. "I know you love her, but Loretta's a piece of junk, scrapped together with cheap parts." I got down on the ground with the two of them. Rossi gazed at me from under her hair. "It's not the bike, Rossi; it's you."

MATTHEW AND I STOOD AT THE EDGE OF

Racetrack Basin for what seemed like forever. I looked around for Rossi. She'd had to get home and get her gear on, and we waited anxiously for her.

"What if she has trouble starting it?" I asked him.

"She knows more about dirt bikes than anyone. She'll be fine." Matthew took a swig from his mayonnaise jar. I had braved sneaking into the kitchen looking like a collapsed mine survivor to get us some water. Wait a minute, I *was* a collapsed mine survivor. Luckily, my grandma hadn't seen me.

"What if she gets dizzy again or sick or—"

"She'll be fine," Matthew repeated. I closed my eyes and took a deep breath, trying to calm my anxiety.

Matthew put a hand on my shoulder. "Seriously, Gus. She's as tough as beef jerky. I'm not worried at all."

I opened my eyes and looked around at all the racers getting ready. I took a sip from my own olive jar of water.

briny: salty

"The race is starting soon," I said. We saw a couple of dirt bikes coming toward us. I groaned. "It's Bo and Jacob."

Matthew folded his arms. Unfolded them. Tugged on his shredded, Twinkie-stained T-shirt. Ran his hand through his sweaty, filthy hair, which still smelled like bat poop.

"Don't worry," I said.

"He's going to kill me."

Bo hopped off his bike in front of us and removed his helmet and goggles. Jacob did the same, but he had lost his smug expression.

"Where is she?" Bo asked. "Is she having bike trouble?" He laughed and smacked Jacob on the shoulder. Jacob smiled, but it looked forced.

Then we heard another bike approaching.

"What?" Bo's mouth hung open. He turned slowly to Matthew. "You gave her your bike?" He drew out each word through clenched teeth.

"I didn't give it to her." Matthew's fingers twisted the bottom of his mangled shirt. "I just lent it to her."

Bo glared at us as Rossi pulled the bike up behind him. She got off and removed her goggles and helmet. She stared at Bo as she passed him, and he slowly turned his glare on her. She didn't take her eyes off him as she walked to me and Matthew. I don't know if Bo noticed, but her lip turned up just a little at one corner.

Mayor Handsome walked up to us. "Looks like vee have a real race today. You guys all ready?" Not only had Mayor Handsome appointed himself mayor of Nowhere, he had also made himself the master of the races. If we weren't careful, I could see him taking over the whole town like some kind of evil overlord. That would actually be pretty exciting.

I peered down into Racetrack Basin and saw the rest of the racers already lining up.

"I'm ready," Rossi said, still watching Bo. He spat on the ground at her feet. She kicked dirt over his spit and turned to us. I handed her my olive jar and she chugged half the water down. "I'll see you guys afterward." She wiped at her mouth.

"After you win," I said. Bo shot me a dirty look. I looked dirty back. Yep. Right on back. I had become quite reckless and daring in the last twenty-four hours.

Rossi breathed in deeply and put her helmet on. She slipped her goggles over her eyes and got on Matthew's bike. She jumped up on the starter. Then she pushed her goggles up. "By the way, Bo," she said over the loud rumble of the motor. He looked at her with the worst seething hatred I'd ever seen. "Those jewels are plastic." She slipped her goggles back over her eyes. "And that gold is fake, too." Then she rode off down to the starting line.

Matthew and I stood there with our mouths hung open. Bo removed the bag of jewels from his pocket and took one out. He bit it in half and spit the pieces on the ground. He threw them down in a rage, then took the piece of gold out of his pocket and threw that down as well. He turned to us. "I'm going to kill you guys," he said through gritted teeth.

Mayor Handsome watched him as he rode away. "Don't vorry. He not killing anybody."

"I'm not so sure about that," Matthew said.

I walked over and picked the gold out of the dirt and stuck it in my pocket. Then I reached for the jewels.

"Don't, Gus."

I looked up at Matthew.

"Just leave them."

Those jewels were one of the only things my dad had ever given me—my dad who had abandoned me. My dad who hadn't called me a single time in seven years. And what was his excuse? What did he need to do that was so important he couldn't take me with him? Rossi's dad was busy saving the world, and he was still here. What was my dad's excuse?

But I wasn't what my dad had done to me. And I was worth more than a bag of worthless plastic jewels. A whole lot more.

I pulled my hand back. And I left them.

Matthew and I watched the riders as they prepared to begin. Rossi was already in line, adjusting her gloves. Bo walked past her with his bike and slammed his shoulder into her back, momentarily throwing her off balance. She managed not to fall and continued adjusting her gloves as though nothing had happened. And I was sure that made Bo madder than anything else she could have done.

Mayor Handsome stood behind the racers with his air horn.

Matthew grabbed his stomach. "I feel sick."

I felt nauseated myself. I looked down at Rossi and shook my head. "Don't worry."

Mayor Handsome blew the air horn and the racers took off.

Right away, Rossi and Bo were out front, Rossi trailing him by a couple of bike lengths. I turned to Matthew. "I don't like to watch from here because you can't see the other side of the track."

We walked along the edge of the basin with our jars of water, watching the racers as we went, until we reached the hill. I pointed at Rossi gliding over the tops of the whoops. The others followed, slowly going over each one. "See?" I said. "She rides like she told you. You have to go faster."

"Yeah, I've never really watched her like this before." Matthew scratched at his matted hair. "It's kind of cool. But she better hurry. Bo is still in front of her."

"She always does this. She trails him for the first three laps, then finally passes on the last. Well, about half of the time. She can't always get around him."

Matthew was staring at me. "What?" I asked.

He shook his head and smiled. "Nothing. You just seem to pay a lot of attention to her."

I shrugged. "Just because she's such a good racer. Everyone likes watching her."

"No. Most people are watching Bo."

As the two of them raced along a berm below us, Matthew said, "Hey, Gus."

"Yeah?"

"If you ever put a diaper on my handlebars again, I'll grind your face into a pile of bat poop."

I tried to hold back my smile. "It's a deal."

Then I reached into my pocket and gripped the pocket watch—the only thing of value I owned. But I didn't really own it. I held it out to Matthew. "Here. This should be yours."

Matthew stared at the pocket watch. "But your dad gave it to you."

"Yeah, well, it wasn't his to give."

Matthew reached out slowly and took it. "You really want to give this to me? Like a present?"

I shrugged. "Not really. It rightfully belongs to you."

Matthew lightly touched the initials engraved on the watch. "No one's ever given me a present before."

I cleared my throat. "Then yes. It's a present."

Matthew put the watch in his pocket. "Thanks,

Gus." He looked down at me, a huge smile on his face, and I swear he looked just the same as he did that day I found him in the bathroom in second grade. *Do you really mean it?*

I sighed and felt my empty pocket where the watch had always been. It seemed I was letting go of a lot of things today.

We continued to watch as Rossi did exactly as I said—she trailed Bo for the first three laps. My queasy stomach was roiling by the last lap. "This is it," Matthew said. "She better do it."

As expected, just as they raced around a berm not far from us, Rossi came up beside Bo. The other racers were nearly half a lap behind them at this point. Only Jacob was fairly close at about a quarter lap behind.

When Bo saw Rossi trying to pass, he gunned his bike, but I knew he wouldn't be able to outrun her— Matthew's bike was faster than Loretta.

Just as Rossi passed him—right in a blind area where I, and Bo no doubt, knew no one could see them but us—Bo reached out and grabbed her handlebars.

extirpate: put an end to something or
   someone; eliminate

He squeezed her front brakes. The bike jolted to a stop, sending her toppling forward. She rolled end over end into the dirt.

Matthew and I were both screaming. I have no idea exactly what words were coming out of our mouths, but I'd estimate they were worth at least a dozen cans of Brussels sprouts.

Rossi was down, but Bo had made a terrible mistake. Not only had he taken his eyes off the track to look at her, but he had taken his hand off his handlebars. He lost his balance as he hit a rut and toppled not far from her.

Rossi lay in the dirt on her back, and I worried she was seriously hurt. "Get up, Rossi!" Matthew and I screamed. As though she had heard us, she raised her head and pushed herself up with one arm.

In the last twenty-four hours, Rossi had scaled a mountain of rubble, fought off bats, run from a mountain lion, gotten chased by javelina, and nearly drowned. Now she had to face Bo.

He marched across the track, and even though I knew it wasn't possible, I swore I could hear every crunch of his boots as they hit the compacted dirt. Rossi stood and faced him, slightly hunched over, one hand held close to her stomach. Before Bo reached her, though, he detoured toward her dirt bike. He lifted a heavy boot, dust flying off of it as though it were smoking, and brought it down hard on one of the wheels.

"My bike!" Matthew cried.

Rossi removed her helmet with the hand not held to her stomach and screamed at him to stop.

I looked frantically at the group of people standing at the starting line—fleas from this distance—but no one could see Rossi and Bo from there. There was no way for me to get down to them.

I looked at the other riders and saw that Jacob was closing in on them. He would pass them soon, and maybe then Bo would stop. But by then it might be too late.

Bo continued stomping the bike. Rossi ran at him. Just as he raised his boot for another crushing blow, she swung her helmet at him hard, causing him to lose his balance and fall back into the dirt.

It wasn't exactly an *usaga*, but I guess Rossi'd had enough trampling in this game as well.

She quickly shoved her helmet and goggles back on and lifted her bike. Before she could get on it, Bo jumped from where he lay on the ground and grabbed her legs, causing her to fall back down.

She struggled to get her legs free, but he held her

firm, doing everything in his power to keep her from getting back on the bike.

And then I saw Jacob rounding the corner. He wasn't going to pass them. He was going to plow right into them. I ran along the edge of the basin, vaguely aware of Matthew running behind me. "They're coming!" I screamed.

ROSSI AND BO SAW JACOB JUST AS HE
rounded the corner at them. Bo released Rossi's legs
and dove to the side of the track and Rossi rolled in
the dirt away from Jacob, who jerked his bike to the
side and wiped out in the silt, sending up a giant dust
cloud.

Rossi wasted no time; she jumped up and limped
back to her bike, her arms held close to her chest.

transcendence: existence beyond the normal
  or physical level; excellence

According to *The Great Ones*, there have been
several instances in which athletes have competed
with serious physical injuries. In 1956, goalie Bert

Trautmann finished the FA Cup with a broken neck. In 1985, football player Ronnie Lott played a game with a crushed finger that later had to be amputated. In 1996, Kerri Strug performed the vault with an injured ankle, ensuring her team won the Olympic gold medal.

And in the year I was about to start eighth grade—though it wouldn't be written about in any book—on that last scorching day of summer vacation, thirteen-year-old Rossi Scott finished a race almost no one in the world knew or cared about with a sprained ankle, a dislocated thumb, and two fractured ribs.

But the handful of people who did know about it cared enough for the whole world.

Bo ran to his own bike and jumped on. And then he was in front of her again. I felt a sinking in my stomach. Every time she tried to pass, he cut her off. I could tell she was hurt. She didn't seem to have the strength left in her to get around him.

As they rounded the last corner, she tried one more time to pass. He blocked her. That was it. There were no more chances.

And then she turned to the right and drove straight into the loose silt.

Matthew threw up his hands. "She's done. That's it. It's over."

The fineness of the silt caused a giant, thick cloud of dust that obscured both Rossi and Bo.

"I can't see what's happening," I cried. "Where are they?" I had seen a lot of riders hit the silt, and a massive dust cloud always erupted when that happened. But this was like a nuclear bomb had gone off.

It felt like hours passed as we ran along the edge of the basin, following the growing cloud, steadily moving toward the finish line like a dust storm headed into town. What was happening in there? The heat pounded down on me to the point where I could no longer run, no longer move, no longer breathe. I used my last remnant of air to call out her name.

She emerged from the cloud and back onto the compacted dirt. She gunned her bike and moved in front of Bo, kicking up dirt right in his face.

Matthew pumped his fist in the air. "Did you see how she just roosted him?"

And then I had the strength to move again. Matthew and I followed her to the end.

Rossi crossed in front of Bo. Just barely. But it was enough.

We ran down to the finish line to meet her. Rossi eased off her bike, removed her helmet and goggles, and limped to us. She was so covered in silt, she looked like she had been dipped in it up to her neck. Her brown eyes sparkled, the outline of her goggles sharp around them.

"You cheated!" Bo spat as he stomped toward us, his boots kicking up so much dust, it looked like he was being followed by a dust devil.

"She did not." I stepped in front of Rossi. "No one ever said you can't ride in the silt. If anyone cheated, it was you. You grabbed her brakes."

"Stay out of this before I put your face in another cactus." He turned to Matthew. "And what's the matter with you?"

Matthew stepped back, putting more distance between himself and Bo. "What?"

"Letting her use your bike. What the heck, man?"

Matthew stood up a little straighter and stuck out his chest. "You shouldn't have gone back on your deal, Bo." He gulped. "You're a liar."

Bo went at him, but now I jumped in front of Matthew. "Leave him alone."

Bo looked surprised for a split second, then he laughed. "Are you going to protect him, you spineless piece of trailer trash?"

"We all live in trailers," I said. "But you're the only trash here, Bo."

And then I did something I had never, ever done before.

I thought of scaling the mountain of rubble in the mine, thinking I would die. I thought of untangling the bat from Rossi's hair, of fighting off the mountain lion with nothing but my backpack, of pulling Rossi from the water when I'd had no strength left. I summoned it all as I pulled back my arm and swung at Bo with everything I had.

And completely missed Bo's face.

Completely. Missed.

By like a whole foot.

And I stumbled a little.

Okay. A lot.

Cut me some slack; I wasn't used to fighting back.

Bo wasted no time. He raised his fist and landed it full-force on my nose. I heard a nauseating crunch and fell to the ground. Warmth trickled down my mouth and chin. I touched it: blood.

I was pretty sure Bo had broken my nose, but I stood back up and faced him. "Is that all you got?" I spit blood on the ground like I was the toughest cowboy in a Western, when really I felt like I was going to throw up.

Bo came at me again, and I swung my arms wildly before he was even close to reaching me. I batted at the empty air, screaming like a madman, my arms two out of control windmills. I was a whirlwind of fists and fury. I was a cyclone of glory and grit. I was a tornado of tough and turpentine. I had my eyes closed, so I'm not totally sure what Bo's reaction was, but I like to think he was at least a tiny bit afraid. Or at least, afraid I had gone insane.

Then we heard a gruff voice shout, "Enough!"

I stopped my threatening display, and we all turned to see Jack walking toward us. "She cheated," Bo whined.

Jack grabbed Bo by his hair. "What's the matter with you? You can't beat a girl at dirt bike racing, and now you're pounding on weaklings?"

I rolled my eyes. *Really?* Did my windmill arms accomplish *nothing*?

Jack let go of Bo's hair, shoving his head at the same time. Bo stumbled and picked up his helmet. "You want to end up in the Center like me?" Jack barked. "Or worse, you want to end up like Dad?"

It was weird to see Bo cower in front of someone. He stared at the ground and shook his head. "Get your stuff together and get your butt home," Jack ordered. Then he looked at Rossi. He nodded slightly to acknowledge her, as though she had earned that nod. He didn't bother with the rest of us. Instead he turned and stomped off, Bo following closely behind.

I knew we'd pick this back up tomorrow at school. But I found I wasn't really all that scared. After all I'd gone through, what more could Bo possibly do to me?

A man walked up to us, and both Rossi's and Matthew's faces went slack-jawed. "You're . . . you're . . . " Rossi mumbled.

The man's face looked equally surprised as he reached his hand out. Rossi held one arm to her chest and stuck the other out to shake his hand. "You're a girl," the man exclaimed.

Rossi shut her mouth, the adulation gone from her face. She tilted her head to the side and furrowed her eyebrows, still shaking the man's hand. "Did you come all the way here to tell me that?"

The man laughed and finally released Rossi's hand. "I think it's awesome you're a girl. Sorry. I was just surprised. I've never seen racing like that from someone so young."

"What are you doing here?" Rossi asked.

"Mayor Handsome told me there were some pretty sweet races going on in this little town. Thought I'd check it out. I love finding talent in strange places."

"You know Mayor Handsome?" Matthew finally piped up.

"Oh yeah," Mayor Handsome said, walking up to us. "Vee go vay back."

"No way," Matthew whispered.

"Vhy you dink I vant to live here?" Mayor Handsome said. "Best dirt bike racing anyvhere. Best climate for my ostriches." He gave us a sly look. "And udder interesting dings."

The man looked at Rossi. "So I'll see you at camp then . . . ?"

"Rossi," she said.

The man laughed. "I love it. I'll see you at camp, Rossi. I'll have your new bike ready for you."

We all watched him walk away. "I can't believe it," Matthew whispered. "No way."

"So who was that?" I said.

Both Rossi and Matthew looked at me, their mouths agape. "Seriously, Gus?" Matthew said. "That was the Breaker himself! I can't believe it!"

I smiled at Rossi. Her eyes absolutely dazzled. "Not impossible," I said.

Mayor Handsome lifted my chin, inspecting my face. He sighed. "I guess vee go to dee hospital now."

MATTHEW, ROSSI, AND I SAT IN THE
waiting room quietly together until Matthew started
to nod off and fell forward out of his chair. He got back
into it, and we giggled together. Matthew rubbed his
head where he'd hit it on the tiled floor. "I want a bed,"
he complained.

"I could sleep for days," I said. "I can't believe we
have to go to school in the morning."

"I can't believe . . ." Rossi began. Then she got up
out of her chair and limped to a man who had just
come through the automatic sliding doors to the emergency room, an anxious look on his face. He wrapped
his arms around her, and Rossi winced. "Hi, Dad."

He relaxed his grip. "What'd you do to yourself?"

"I crashed."

He put his hands on her shoulders and held her at arm's length. "My Rossi? Crash? I don't believe it."

"She was sabotaged," Matthew said. "But she still won."

Rossi's dad looked at Matthew, his eyes widening in surprise at his appearance. He turned his attention back to Rossi. "That sounds more like it." He scanned her up and down, probably taking in her dirt-stained, ripped clothing and many scrapes and scratches. "Are you okay?"

She nodded.

"I thought maybe you'd spent the night at the Navarros' place when I got home late last night, but Mrs. Navarro informs me that's not the case." He looked at Rossi expectantly, but she stayed quiet. "She says you have quite a story to tell me." He raked a hand through his dark hair. "About where you were last night."

A woman in scrubs walked into the waiting room just then and called Rossi's name.

Rossi looked at her father. "Do you want to go in with me?"

"I thought I'd at least stay long enough to make sure you're okay," he told her. He glanced at us. "But first I want to have a word with these two grubby guys."

Matthew shifted in his seat as Rossi disappeared through the doors with the nurse. "Uh-oh," he muttered.

Mr. Scott stood over us, his rumpled suit covered in dust smudges from hugging his daughter. "You two look like you've been in battle."

Matthew stuck his chest out. "We have."

Mr. Scott rubbed at his forehead. "You were with Rossi last night?"

We both nodded.

He let out a tired sigh. "I don't even know who you are."

"We're Rossi's friends," I told him.

"I didn't know she'd made friends."

"I think there's a lot you don't know," I said.

He stopped rubbing at his forehead. He looked shocked at my statement. He opened his mouth to say something, but a sweaty, pink-cheeked baby let out a scream a few seats down.

Matthew and I jumped at the sound.

"As much as I'd like to stay here talking to you two," Mr. Scott said over the wails of the baby, "I'd better go see how Rossi's doing before I'm needed back at work."

He started to walk away, but I summoned all my

courage and cried out, "She needs you, too, you know." I was kind of impressed with the level of attitude I'd managed to convey.

He halted. Then he turned around and walked back to us. He looked down at me. "I don't think you know her very well. My Rossi is the strongest person I know. She can fend for herself. She doesn't need anybody."

The mom shoved a pacifier into the baby's mouth and it finally quieted. I stared at Mr. Scott. "Needing her dad doesn't make her weak."

His head shot back in surprise at my words. The baby spit the pacifier out, and it landed at his feet. He stared at it a moment before picking it up and handing it back to the woman, who mumbled a tired thanks.

He turned back to me, a pained look on his face, as the baby started wailing again. "Thanks for the tip," he finally said softly before rejoining his daughter on the other side of the doors.

headway: progress, especially when
  circumstances make it slow or difficult

3:00 PM

THE DOCTOR MOVED MY HEAD GENTLY from side to side, carefully examining my mutilated face. "You should see the other guy," I told him. He gave me a skeptical look. I lowered my eyes. "Yeah, he's completely fine."

"Your nose is broken." Now that was a shock, especially since my nose looked like it had been stapled sideways to my cheek. And then there was the bucket of blood that had come out. And, you know, the pain. "I'll have to set it."

I squeezed my eyes shut and, still humming from my earlier adrenaline rush, told him, "Just do it."

He pushed my nose to one side, and there was another crunch.

excruciation: severe pain; agony; torture

I whimpered loud enough that I was sure Matthew and Rossi could hear me from wherever they were—whatever gains I had made with my bravery earlier were probably being erased.

I swooned to one side, and the doctor held me up. "You okay?"

The room spun. I turned my head and vomited on the table. At least it was covered in paper, but I felt bad about not having attempted to make it to the sink or trash can.

I wiped at my mouth. "Sorry."

"It's okay," the doctor said, like this was a normal occurrence in the emergency room. I guess it probably was. He gave me instructions for caring for my broken nose. A nurse cleaned me up and let me rinse my mouth out in the sink.

I found Rossi and Matthew waiting for me in the hallway. "Everything okay?" Rossi said, her face creased with worry.

"No big deal." I shrugged casually. "Just a broken nose. I totally handled it."

Matthew raised an eyebrow at me, then smiled. "Of course you did."

Rossi's ankle was wrapped with tape. I saw the crutches propped against the wall. "What did they say about your ankle?"

"Sprained. I'll be off it for a while."

Her hand was also wrapped in tape. "What about your hand?"

"Dislocated thumb."

"And the doctor says a couple of her ribs are fractured," Matthew said. "But there's nothing they can do about that."

My broken nose didn't seem so tough anymore.

"Where's your dad?" I asked.

"Just left," Rossi said. "Back to work. As usual."

Jessie's mom walked up to us. "You can see him now." We started to enter the room, but she stopped me. "Not you, Gus."

I faced her. She was visibly shocked at my appearance. I must have been quite a sight—all spots and blood and dirt and black eyes. "Now what happened to *you*?" She threw her hands up in exasperation. "Jessie's been shot and smells like he slept in a sewer, Rossi is incredibly beat up, and you look like you've been put through a dirt blender."

"Just got in a fight." I pushed my shoulders back. "I *almost* didn't lose," I said, maybe a little arrogantly.

"But what happened last night? I just about called the police this morning when I couldn't find Jessie."

"What did he tell you?"

She shook her head. "Oh no. Nuh-uh. What's your story?"

I didn't have the energy to lie. I told her a very abbreviated version of what had happened, leaving out the part about the gold.

She shook her head. "Yep. That's just what he told me. You know, you guys could have gotten yourselves killed. Whatever possessed you to be so reckless?"

I turned my head and saw Rossi sitting on the bed next to Jessie. She was nodding at something he was saying to her. I smiled. "Justice." I put my hands on my hips and faced Mrs. Navarro. "I had to fight for justice."

Mrs. Navarro rolled her eyes and waved a hand at me. "You're something else, Gus. Listen, I'm very sorry, but I'll have to tell your grandma about all this."

I groaned. She'd probably nail my window shut. "No," I pleaded with Mrs. Navarro.

"Yes," she said firmly. "The hospital will be calling her anyway. How did you plan on explaining this?" She gestured wildly at my entire body and face.

"I kind of hoped she wouldn't notice."

Mrs. Navarro laughed. "Even if she miraculously

didn't notice that you've turned into steak *picado* over-night, she's going to notice the hospital bill when it shows up in her mailbox." Her face fell. "I don't know how we're going to pay all these bills—Jessie's and Rossi's and yours. None of us can afford this." She closed her eyes and squeezed the bridge of her nose. "I can't even think about it right now.

"Don't worry," I said. "We'll figure out a way to pay for it."

She raised an eyebrow at me. "We?"

I smiled. "It will work out."

"I've missed you, Gus." She ruffled my filthy hair, then looked at her hand in disgust. "You really are something else." She wiped her hand off on her jeans. "All right, you'd better go in and see him. He's going to be okay and can leave as soon as they discharge him. Of course you'd think he shot off his entire leg by the way he was acting when he came in here."

"Typical Jessie," I said.

"Typical Jessie," she agreed. I watched as she walked down the hallway to a desk where a woman handed her a clipboard with some paperwork to fill out.

I stepped into the room. The three of them were laughing. "I'm not a whole man anymore, Gus," Jessie announced. "I have a missing limb."

I looked in shock at his foot. "But, I thought . . ."

"Pinky toe, man," Jessie said with pride, raising his fatly wrapped foot. "I lost my pinky toe. And since it's probably stuck to the wall of the cave, I will just have to go without. You think the girls will dig it?"

"Yeah. Maybe you can even get a peg pinky toe," I said.

Jessie laughed. "Just like a pirate. *Arrrrr*."

"Or a Viking," said Rossi.

"How about you?" said Jessie to me.

"Just a broken nose. No biggie."

"And Rossi kicked Bo's butt." Jessie raised a triumphant fist in the air. "Man, I wish I could have seen it."

"It was awesome," I said.

"Completely awesome," said Matthew.

Jessie smiled and shook his head. "I hate that I wasn't there."

Then, unexpectedly, Jessie put his face in his hands and cried. The three of us glanced at one another, not knowing what to do. Rossi patted Jessie's back. "It's okay," she said. "You don't need your pinky toe."

"Sorry, guys." Jessie wiped at his nose. "I don't know why I'm crying." He started laughing through his tears. "Just everything that's happened, I guess."

Like I said—total lightweight.

4:00 PM

MRS. NAVARRO DROVE US BACK TO

Nowhere. With all the crutches, it was a tight squeeze in the old Malibu. She stopped the car in front of the Nowhere Market and Ostrich Farm. "Mayor Handsome told me you could all have free Popsicles in honor of Rossi's win."

"And Jessie's missing toe," added Rossi.

"And Gus's broken nose," said Jessie.

"And Matthew's sacrifice," I said. We all smiled at one another.

"I'll tell you who *won't* be getting free Popsicles," Matthew said, and we snickered.

Mrs. Navarro got out of the car and helped Jessie out of the front seat.

The three of us didn't budge in the back. "I can't move," Matthew said. "I think my body just died."

"I know," I said. Every single part of me ached. But it somehow also felt alive—more alive than I had ever felt. And I decided I'd rather feel pain and exhaustion than whatever it was I had been feeling day after day before last night. I finally pushed myself out of the car and helped Rossi out.

"What were guys doing in there?" Jessie said, already standing on the front porch on one foot, two Popsicles in his hands, two in Mrs. Navarro's. "You weren't making out, were you?"

My face grew hot and Jessie laughed. "Gus, you're so red. You totally wish."

I gritted my teeth. "I have no interest in making out with Matthew."

Mrs. Navarro looked at her watch as Matthew and I helped Rossi up the steps. "I'm going to go finish up some work at the scrapyard. Be back in an hour?"

Jessie nodded and kissed his mom's cheek.

She turned to us. "Stay put."

The four of us sat on the bench on the porch of the Nowhere Market and Ostrich Farm, licking our Popsicles, already melting in the heat.

"I guess I'll be hearing all about it as soon as I get home," I said.

"Not me," Rossi said. "My dad won't have time."

"I think he'll make time for this," I said.

Rossi raised an eyebrow at me. "How do you know?"

I shrugged. "Just a feeling."

"Sorry I had to rat you guys out," Jessie said. "My ma is the world's best interrogator."

Matthew's throat bobbed. "My mom thinks I spent the night at Bo's. Did your mom call her, Jessie?"

I stared at Matthew. He gripped his Popsicle stick so hard, his knuckles were as white as his color-drained face.

Maybe he wasn't so used to it after all.

Jessie grinned at him. "Why would she? You weren't even with us last night. Like you said, you spent the night at Bo's."

Relief washed over Matthew's face and the color returned. He took a big bite of his Popsicle. "You know," he said. "Maybe we could all sit together at lunch tomorrow."

I glanced at Rossi. She had sat by herself at lunchtime all last year, but she smiled now. "Okay."

Jessie licked at his bright orange and red Popsicle. "Yeah, I could take a break from Ramiro's group." He smiled at me. "Make some time for old friends." He looked at Matthew. "And new ones, too." Then his face fell. "But Bo will be after us now, you know."

I gulped. "I know."

"He'll never forget what I did," Matthew said, Popsicle juice dripping down his hand and onto his ripped pants. "I don't think he'll be happy until I pay for it."

I held my hand out. "We stick together. That will be our best defense."

Jessie put his hand on mine. "Stick together." Matthew did the same.

I looked at Rossi. She stared at our hands. Maybe Rossi didn't want to be here in Nowhere. Who did? And maybe all she really did need was her bike and a desolate Mexican desert, but that was still a long time away. In the meantime . . .

"Stick together." She placed her hand on the pile.

"Maybe we'll survive eighth grade," Jessie said.

"We'll totally survive," I assured him. "I know we will."

We dropped our hands and went back to slurping our Popsicles. "Oh, and we have to let Louis sit with us," I said. "I know he spits a lot and all, but I can't abandon the poor guy. He'd be dead in about a week."

"Our table has an open-door policy," Rossi said. "Anyone is welcome."

Our table.

The wind suddenly picked up, and Matthew rubbed at his eyes. "Haboob's coming," he said.

haboob: a violent wind blowing in summer,
   bringing sand from the desert

We all laughed. Popsicle juice shot out of Jessie's mouth and dribbled down his chin.

You didn't need to be a vocabulary expert to know what that word meant here in Arizona, and no one could resist the urge to use it when the opportunity presented itself.

As I licked my Popsicle, I thought about what I had been doing twenty-four hours ago. Had Bo really been pushing my face into the cholla? It didn't seem possible. Like another life. It really was another life.

I heard snoring, and I turned my head. Both Matthew and Jessie had fallen asleep, and Matthew had his head laid on Jessie's shoulder, his mouth wide open, already dripping Popsicle-tinted saliva on him. Jessie had his head laid on Rossi's shoulder with pretty much the same expression as Matthew's. Both of their Popsicles were melting into big, dark, wet spots on their already destroyed pants.

Rossi chuckled beside me, and I laughed softly with her. "I'm going to give him my old bike," she said.

"What? Who?"

"Jessie. He needs a new one."

"But I thought you loved your bike."

"I do, but I realized something today during the race while I was riding Matthew's."

"What's that?"

"My old bike's a trasheep."

We giggled together. "Besides," she said, "I'm going to need a better bike to work with if I'm going to teach you how to ride."

My stomach tightened. "Really?"

"Yep."

The wind suddenly picked up. A couple of our Popsicle wrappers blew onto the porch and tumbled down the steps, joining the rest of the garbage that lined the roadside. "Hey, what do you think is in the circle?" Rossi asked.

I tilted my head a little. "What circle?"

"The circled area on the map."

A piece of dust blew into my eye and I rubbed at it. "I have no idea."

"You know, no one knows for sure they found the gold in the mine."

"What are you saying? They might have found the gold in the cave?"

"Perhaps. And perhaps there's still more in there."

The wind blew Rossi's hair all around her face and some of it stuck to her Popsicle.

I laughed. "Well, let's go check it out."

She yawned and picked her hair away from the Popsicle. "Maybe another day."

I nodded and grinned at her. "Another day."

We sat there quietly licking our Popsicles, the only sounds our slurps and Matthew's and Jessie's snores. More dust blew into my eyes.

"Hey, Gus," Rossi said.

"Hm?" I blinked and wiped at my eyes.

"Thanks for saving my life."

I stopped wiping at my eyes and looked at her. "You're welcome."

"You're quite heroic, aren't you?"

I shrugged. "Oh, I don't know about that. I just know CPR."

She smiled. "You know about a lot of things." She raised her good hand. I put mine in it, and she closed her fingers over it. "Even Steven."

"Even Steven."

Rossi's smile vanished as she continued holding my hand. The sky suddenly darkened as the wind continued to pick up. She stared at me, her hair blowing around her. "It's Loretta," she finally whispered.

"Don't worry. We'll get the wheels fixed before you give her to Jessie."

"No." Rossi laid her head on my shoulder and let out a long sigh. "My motorcycle doesn't have a name."

A moment later, her Popsicle was melting into soup in her lap.

I leaned my head on top of Rossi's and gazed out at the town of Nowhere, the poorest town in Arizona and the least livable town in the entire United States. An actual tumbleweed blew across the crumbling road in front of us. In the hazy distance, a giant wall of dust was heading our way. A piece of Rossi's hair swirled in the wind and tickled my face as she snored softly beside me. I breathed in deeply and smelled creosote. That meant it was raining *somewhere*.

felicity: great happiness; bliss

ACKNOWLEDGMENTS

Thank you so much to my editor, Christina Pulles, for her wisdom and guidance. Thank you to Ryan Thomann, Heather Kelly, and João Neves for designing a gorgeous jacket and cover. And to everyone at Sterling for the constant support: Theresa Thompson, Hannah Reich, Ardi Alspach, Sari Lampert Murray, Maha Khalil, Chris Vaccari, and the entire sales team. I can't imagine a better home for my stories.

Thank you to my agent, Shannon Hassan, for patiently listening to all my ideas. Thank you to my sensitivity readers for helping me create authentic characters. Thank you to all of the booksellers, librarians, and educators who share my books with children. To my early readers and writer friends, especially the members of AZ YA Writers. To my husband for being my number one cheerleader, beta reader, and inspiration giver. To my children for filling my life with joy. To my mother for always believing in me. To God for sending me on this incredible path. And, last but not least, thank you to all of my amazing readers, especially the young ones.

24 Hours in NOWHERE

Discussion Questions

1 The four main characters in the novel have very different home lives. Which character's home life is most like yours? In what ways?

2 Why is Bo a bully? What do you think you should do when you see someone being bullied?

3 What does Rossi mean when she asks Gus if he's going to let someone else's actions define him? Has anyone ever made you feel bad about yourself? How do you handle those feelings?

4 What examples of teamwork can you find in the story? Do you think any of the four characters could have survived the events alone?

5 Why are Gus, Rossi, Jessie, and Matthew so poor? Have they made choices that caused their poverty or made it worse?

6 Rossi collects scrap metal from the desert and sells it to the scrap yard so she can maintain her dirt bike. What things of yours do you have to pay for yourself? How do you earn the money?

7 Do you think better-off people tend to look down on others who are poverty-stricken? How do you view others who have less than you?

8 The novel is told in the first person, from Gus's point of view. How do you think the story would change if it were told from Rossi, Jessie, or Matthew's point of view? What if it were told from Bo's point of view?

9 Give an example of a time when Gus, Rossi, Jessie, and Matthew each sacrifice something to help someone.

Gus often uses humor when talking about his living situation. Why?

Why does Gus believes acing the SAT is his only way to get into college? What does this reveal about challenges people born into poverty face? What does it mean to be born with privilege?

 Think about the setting the author has chosen for the novel. How does it affect the way you read the story?

 Why did the author choose to tell the story in an hour-by-hour format?

The Gus we meet at the beginning of the story is different from the Gus at the end. Compare and contrast the ways he has changed and the ways he remains the same. How have the other characters changed?

How do the relationships among the four main characters change from the time they enter the mine until they finally emerge from the cave? What do you think caused these changes?

READ ON FOR A PEEK!

WHEN I WAS LITTLE, A KID POINTED at me on the playground and shouted, "Her arms fell off!" then ran away screaming in terror to his mom, who had to cuddle him on her lap and rub his head for like ten minutes to get him to calm down. I think, up until then, I hadn't thought about the idea that my arms must have *actually* fallen off at some point in my life. I had never really thought about not having arms at all.

My missing arms weren't an issue for me or my parents. I never once heard either of them say, "Oh, no, Aven can't possibly do that because that's only for armed people," or "Poor Aven is so helpless without arms," or "Maybe Aven can do that one day, you know, if she ever grows some arms." They always said things like, "You'll have to do this differently from other people, but you can manage," and "I know this is challenging. Keep trying," and "You're capable of anything, Aven."

I had never realized just how different I was until the day that horrible kid shouted about my arms having fallen off. For the first time I found myself aware of my total armlessness, and I guess I felt like I was sort of naked all of a sudden. So I, too, ran to my mom, and she scooped me up and carried me away from the park, allowing my tears and snot to soak her shirt.

As she drove us home that day, I sat whimpering in my car seat and asked her what had happened to my arms and why they'd fallen off. She told me they hadn't fallen off; I was just born like that. I asked her how I could get some new ones. She said I couldn't. I wailed in despair, and she told me to stop crying because having arms was totally overrated. I didn't know what *overrated* meant at the time because, like I said, I was really little and so was my brain. I kind of figured it out over the next few days, though, because my parents were constantly saying things like, "Coloring this picture with my hands is okay, but if only I could color it with my feet like Aven. Now that would be fantastic," and "Eating spaghetti with my arms is just so boring. I wish I could eat it with my feet," and "The only person I know who can pick their nose with their toes is Aven. She sure is a special little girl." Dad even went so far as to ask Mom if there were any arm-removal services in the area.

Growing up, I could do most everything everyone else with arms could do: eating cereal, brushing my teeth and hair, getting dressed, and yes, even wiping my own bottom. I know you're instantly wondering how I do it, and maybe I'll tell you later . . . maybe. Until then, you'll just have to live in suspense.

Sure, these things take longer for me. Sometimes they take *a lot* longer. Sometimes I have to use a special tool like a hook or a strap or something like that. And every now and then I want to scream in frustration and kick a pillow until the stuffing comes out because it's taken me twenty minutes to get my pants buttoned. But I *can* button my pants.

I think I can do all these things because my parents have always encouraged me to figure things out on my own—well, more like *made* me figure things out on my own. I suppose if they had always done everything for me, I would be helpless without them. But they didn't, and I'm not. And now that I'm

thirteen years old, I don't need much help with anything. True story.

When I started kindergarten, the kids were a little weirded out by my lack of armage. I got asked just
about every day what had happened to my arms, as
well as a billion other silly questions—like how do I
make farting noises with my armpits when I don't
have arms or hands . . . or pits. And how do I play
dress-up—which I tried showing them and ended up
with a poofy pink tutu thing stuck around my head for
about five minutes before the teacher finally noticed
and helped me pull it down to my waist.

I got so tired of telling them the same boring story
about being born without arms that I started making
stuff up. It was stinking hilarious. I knew from the first
moment I told a girl my arms had burned off in a fire, I
had found a great hobby: making up stories. I loved the
way her eyes grew wide with shock and the way her voice
went all high-pitched with excitement as she asked me a
bunch more questions about my charred arms.

Her: "What kind of fire accident?"

Me: "A wild forest fire burning out of control!"

Her: "Where?"

Me: "In the mountains of Tanzania." (I honestly
didn't know where Tanzania was or if it had any

mountains. I think I had heard the name in an episode of *Scooby-Doo* or something.)

Her: "How old were you?"

Me: "Just a helpless baby. My mom barely rescued me in time. She pulled me from my burning crib and raced out of our flaming village, leaving a trail of fire all the way down the mountain as my arms burned to a crisp! They looked like two pieces of bacon by the time we got to the village hospital!"

Another kid standing nearby: "Cooked or uncooked?"

So I kind of traumatized her and had to have a meeting with my parents and the teacher later about my story. My parents squinted their eyes and pursed their lips and nodded their heads as the teacher told them, "Um, Aven told another child that her arms burned off in a wildfire in the mountains of Tanzania." She peered at them over her glasses, frowning. "She also mentioned something about bacon."

I had never seen such serious looks on my parents' faces before, like they were concentrating so hard on being serious, their heads might explode if they blinked. They said seriously they would talk to me about it and shook the teacher's hand seriously and gave me serious looks as we walked seriously out of school. But I could tell they weren't mad because all the way home one of them would softly snort and then the other would giggle and then the other would shake from laughing but trying not to laugh out loud and on and on like that all the way home.

They later told me just to be truthful so I didn't upset any other kids. And I did for a long time. But then one day in fifth grade, we had a new kid come to our school. (I had gone to the same school since kindergarten, so all my friends knew I was just born with no arms.) When I sat down at lunch with this kid, he said, "Whoa! What happened to your arms?"

All my friends were looking at me, and what can I say? It exploded out of me like an overfilled water balloon. I told him this crazy story about how I had rescued a puppy that had been tied to the train tracks just in time before a train nearly ran over it—just in time for the puppy . . . but not for my poor, flattened arms.

You should have seen the look on this kid's face—priceless. My best friend, Emily, burst out laughing and my friend Kayla spit chocolate milk across the table. The new kid realized it was a joke and started laughing, too.

Pretty soon everyone was constantly asking me, "Hey, Aven! Where'd your arms go?" And I would have a new story to tell. Over time my stories got more and more ridiculous: alligator wrestling in the Everglades in Florida, freak roller coaster accidents, skydiving trips gone wrong. I made my stories as ridiculous as possible so people would always know I was joking.

I grew up with those kids. I never felt out of place or anything like that. My armlessness wasn't strange or weird to them because, like I said, I had always gone to the same school.

I never imagined my parents would make me leave. I never thought they would make me move all the way to Arizona and go to a new school right after starting eighth grade.

Then again, I never imagined I would save the Old West, perform for an audience in the desert, and solve a mystery. You'd be surprised at all I'm capable of, though. Even without arms.

THE DAY DAD TOLD ME HE WANTED

to apply for a job as a theme park manager in Arizona, I thought it was quite possible aliens had taken over his brain—either aliens or the government. I knew from my great-grandma the government was capable of dreadful things. She was always saying stuff like, "If the public only knew what the government was up to, there would be a revolution!" and pumping her spotted, wrinkled fist in the air. I wasn't completely sure why an eighty-six-year-old woman who lived in a trailer in Kansas was the only person privy to this top-secret information, but she *clearly* was. So I wouldn't put it past the government to insert some kind of mind-control chip into Dad's brain and force him to run a crumbling theme park in the desert.

My parents discussed it with me one night over a dinner of buttered noodles, my favorite meal. Oh, man—I just realized they deliberately buttered me up with buttered noodles.

"So I got an email from a guy by the name of Joe Cavanaugh," Dad said over his noodles. "He owns a place called Stagecoach Pass."

"What's that?" I asked, slurping up a noodle.

"It's this western-themed amusement park in Arizona. I guess he found my résumé on one of the job sites where I posted it. Anyway, he invited me to apply for the position of general manager at the park."

"He must have been impressed with your résumé, Mister-Big-Time-Restaurant-Manager," said Mom.

"Well," said Dad, "I'm not really sure how managing a restaurant relates to managing an entire theme park, but I guess a huge part of their business is this steakhouse there, so that's probably why he contacted me."

"Are you going to apply?" I asked.

"It does sound interesting," said Dad.

I scowled. "Arizona is really far away."

"Don't forget you were born there, Sheebs," Dad said. "We spent a lot of time there during your adoption, and we really liked it. We even thought it might be a great place to retire one day. The winter was so beautiful—warm and sunny. I'm sick of icy winters."

"What's the summer like?" I asked.

Mom grimaced. "I've heard it's kind of like the surface of the sun."

"It could be an exciting adventure." Dad waggled his eyebrows at me. "Swimming and soccer all year long."

I glared at my noodles. "I don't think I want to play soccer on the surface of the sun."

"Come on," said Dad. "You're such a pro, you could play soccer anywhere."

"Stop trying to entice me," I said. "You haven't even applied yet."

"Well, if it's okay with you, I'd like to."

On the one hand, the thought of leaving Kansas, and the only home I could ever remember, sounded worse than anything. On the other, Dad had lost his job nearly six months earlier, when the restaurant he'd been managing went out of business. He really needed this.

"It's okay with me," I mumbled, feeling like I might cry.

Dad applied. And then he and Mom were invited to go to Arizona for an interview and to check the place out. And then they were invited to stay and run the theme park together. Turns out it was more of a two-person job.

And so we sold off a ton of our furniture and donated the junk we didn't need and packed the rest of our belongings into a giant pod that would magically disappear from Kansas and magically reappear in Arizona a week later. We drove our old car over a thousand miles westward across the country, praying the entire time we wouldn't break down.

We managed to make it in one single long day without stopping at a hotel until we got to Phoenix. By the time we arrived, Dad's eyes looked like Atomic Fireballs and Mom's hair looked like she'd taken a spin in a hairspray cyclone.

Early the next morning, we drove by the giant covered wagon with **STAGECOACH PASS** printed on it in large brown block letters, and I saw the park for the first time.

Then I knew for sure the government and mind-control chips were involved.

WE PARKED IN THE LARGE DIRT

parking lot and got out of the car. I squinted from the bright, hot sun. Had the sun been this bright in Kansas? I didn't think so.

I looked around. I'd never seen so much brown before—not a patch of grass anywhere. Did grass even exist in Arizona? Again, I didn't think so.

We walked over the compacted dirt toward the entrance, which wasn't closed up, even though the park wasn't open yet—I guess they weren't too worried about people sneaking in. A lizard skittered across the dirt in front of me, and I jumped back.

The dirt. Never. Ended. There were no sidewalks or grass or paved anything at Stagecoach Pass—just dirt and old wooden buildings with old wooden steps and old wooden porches that looked like they might collapse at any time.

"Good morning!" a cheerful, gray-mustached man greeted us from one of these porches. He wore a cowboy hat and held a mug of something steamy. Coffee? In this heat?

"Good morning," Mom and Dad said at the same time.

"Nice to see you again, Gary," said Mom. I looked at her. "He's the one who interviewed us," she whispered to me. "He's the accountant for the park."

Gary walked down the steps. "And this must be Aven."

"Our one and only," Dad said, squeezing his arm around me.

I gave Gary a polite smile. He seemed nice enough, even though his gray mustache was awfully pointy.

"Well," Gary said, tossing his coffee on the dirt, where it dried in about two seconds, "I bet you're tired after your long trip. I'll take you up to the apartment."

As we trudged toward our new living quarters, which were apparently located right over the steakhouse, Dad asked, "So when do we get to meet Joe Cavanaugh?"

"Oh, no one ever meets Joe," said Gary. "Not around here much."

"That's strange," said Mom. "A business owner who doesn't visit his own business?"

Gary smiled and tilted his hat at her. "That's why Joe needs good managers, ma'am."

Mom and Dad had described the apartment as a cozy but humble little place. They weren't kidding about the cozy. Or the humble. Or the little.

Gary and a few other men from the park (all dressed like cowboys), carried our stuff up from the car. After Mom and I finished putting away my suitcase of bare necessities, she said to me, "Why don't you go out and explore, honey?"

"What's there to explore?"

"Tons of stuff," she said. "There's a gold mine, and a gift shop, and a museum, and a soda shop. You could get yourself an ice cream." She looked at her watch. "It won't be open for a half hour, though."

So I went out and explored. For about five minutes. The heat got more and more intense with every second until I was forced into the air-conditioned museum.

The museum was actually more like a room—just one room with picture-covered walls and a few "artifacts" in glass cases. These artifacts included a collection of stone arrowheads, some broken Navajo pottery pieces, a pistol from the 1800s, a pair of old spurs, and a genuine dead tarantula with an information board that shared facts like, tarantulas have no teeth, so they use their venom to liquefy their prey and suck up the liquid nastiness directly into their stomachs. How awesome is that?

I scanned the framed photographs on the walls, the old wooden floorboards creaking under my feet. Most of the pictures were black and white, taken a long time ago when Stagecoach Pass first opened. It looked like it was quite the place back then—crowds and rodeos and even parades on Main Street. Then I came to an empty space on the wall, where it seemed a picture had been removed. The nameplate beneath the empty space had been left up and said *The Cavanaughs, Stagecoach Pass, 2004.*

I looked around at the rest of the photos and each of their nameplates, but I couldn't find any more of the Cavanaughs. I thought about what Gary had said: *No one ever meets Joe.* And I wondered why.

"There you are," Dad said from behind me. "I've been looking for you."

I turned around. "Just getting some cool air."

"Don't worry." Dad wiped the sweat from his forehead. "It will cool down soon. Guess what?"

"What?"

"The rodeo arena is all closed down, so I thought we could set up a soccer goal out there and practice."

"That sounds great."

"You want to go kick the ball around now?"

"Isn't it too hot?"

"Never. Plus, we can keep cool with ice cream."

"What if I get a sunburn?"

"They have sunblock in the gift shop."

I smiled. "You have an answer for everything, don't you?"

Dad put an arm around me and led me into the gift shop. "Of course. Didn't you know that dads know everything?"

I snorted as he picked out a small tube of sunblock from a rack. "I'd like to be there when you tell Mom that."